An Innocent Imposter
Sheila Rabe

**ZEBRA BOOKS
KENSINGTON PUBLISHING CORP.**

ZEBRA BOOKS are published by

Kensington Publishing Corp.
850 Third Avenue
New York, NY 10022

Copyright © 1995 by Sheila Rabe

All rights reserved. No part of this book may be reproduced in any form or by any means without the prior written consent of the Publisher, excepting brief quotes used in reviews.

If you purchased this book without a cover you should be aware that this book is stolen property. It was reported as "unsold and destroyed" to the Publisher and neither the Author nor the Publisher has received any payment for this "stripped book."

Zebra and the Z logo Reg. U.S. Pat. & TM Off.

First Printing: May, 1995

Printed in the United States of America

AN UNEXPECTED ATTRACTION

The earl returned his attention to Susan. "How is it I find you alone with yet another man?"

"It was not my idea, I assure you," she said.

"Oh?"

"It was Mr. Caine's. I am afraid he still thinks me a governess in his house."

"As, yes. Miss Layne, the governess."

"Yes, Miss Layne the governess," sighed Susan.

"You are a most convincing actress," said the earl grudgingly.

"Your lordship." Susan laid a pleading hand on his arm.

He looked at it in a detached manner, rather like someone observing a ladybug on his sleeve. Then he took it in his and raised it for a closer examination. "The first two times I saw you, you were biting your thumbnail," he said. "When did you stop biting your thumbnail, Arabella?"

"I have never bitten my fingernails," Susan replied.

The earl raised his gaze from her hand to her mouth. "Your voice. You are still speaking with it lowered. I rather like it," he added absently.

Susan looked at him, mesmerized. "Do you?" she whispered.

"I . . . do." Slowly, as if drawn by some magnetic force, the earl's lips lowered toward hers . . .

ZEBRA'S REGENCY ROMANCES
DAZZLE AND DELIGHT

A BEGUILING INTRIGUE (4441, $3.99)
by Olivia Sumner

Pretty as a picture Justine Riggs cared nothing for propriety. She dressed as a boy, sat on her horse like a jockey, and pondered the stars like a scientist. But when she tried to best the handsome Quenton Fletcher, Marquess of Devon, by proving that she was the better equestrian, he would try to prove Justine's antics were pure folly. The game he had in mind was seduction — never imagining that he might lose his heart in the process!

AN INCONVENIENT ENGAGEMENT (4442, $3.99)
by Joy Reed

Rebecca Wentworth was furious when she saw her betrothed waltzing with another. So she decides to make him jealous by flirting with the handsomest man at the ball, John Collinwood, Earl of Stanford. The "wicked" nobleman knew exactly what the enticing miss was up to — and he was only too happy to play along. But as Rebecca gazed into his magnificent eyes, her errant fiancé was soon utterly forgotten!

SCANDAL'S LADY (4472, $3.99)
by Mary Kingsley

Cassandra was shocked to learn that the new Earl of Lynton was her childhood friend, Nicholas St. John. After years at sea and mixed feelings Nicholas had come home to take the family title. And although Cassandra knew her place as a governess, she could not help the thrill that went through her each time he was near. Nicholas was pleased to find that his old friend Cassandra was his new next door neighbor, but after being near her, he wondered if mere friendship would be enough . . .

HIS LORDSHIP'S REWARD (4473, $3.99)
by Carola Dunn

As the daughter of a seasoned soldier, Fanny Ingram was accustomed to the vagaries of military life and cared not a whit about matters of rank and social standing. So she certainly never foresaw her *tendre* for handsome Viscount Roworth of Kent with whom she was forced to share lodgings, while he carried out his clandestine activities on behalf of the British Army. And though good sense told Roworth to keep his distance, he couldn't stop from taking Fanny in his arms for a kiss that made all hearts equal!

Available wherever paperbacks are sold, or order direct from the Publisher. Send cover price plus 50¢ per copy for mailing and handling to Penguin USA, P.O. Box 999, c/o Dept. 17109, Bergenfield, NJ 07621. Residents of New York and Tennessee must include sales tax. DO NOT SEND CASH.

For Rana

One

Dismissed without references! Miss Susan Layne sat, oblivious to the other passengers milling about the inn yard waiting for the Eclipse, and wondered how she'd ever be able to tell her mama. To return home from her first post in disgrace, and undeserved disgrace at that— oh, it did not bear thinking of!

If only she'd had the good fortune to be plain, then she would have succeeded quite well as a governess. Alas, Susan was not plain. She had eyes the color of bluebells and a small, straight nose. And although her mouth was a little too wide to be a perfect rosebud, her mama had always been quick to assure her that it was still a perfectly nice mouth and really didn't mar her beauty in the least. Even her hair was lovely; "The golden color that is so often admired by gentlemen," Mama often said.

Susan sighed glumly. If she had been a lady of wealth and title, her looks would have done her some good. But her papa had been a soldier, her mama a genteel female who ran a school for young ladies, and the pittance she and her mother lived on after her father's death had no more allowed her to move in high circles than had her parents' social position. Her mama had thought that if Susan found employment in a great house, some young nobleman was bound to see her and fall hopelessly in love. But things had turned out quite the opposite. Her fine looks had caused her to lose her governess-position.

Really! Susan fumed. It had been very unfair of Lady Wight to blame her, as if she had sought out the future Lord Wight. Why ever would she seek the company of a pimply young man who was forever trying to back her into corners and kiss her?

Now, she supposed, she would have to accept the vicar's son. The thought of marrying the scrawny Abner Smedly and finishing her life in genteel poverty, doing noble deeds held no appeal for her. Not that Susan had any objection to doing noble deeds. But she'd had enough of being shabby-genteel.

A new thought occurred to her. What if news of her disgrace got out? Even Mr. Smedly would not have her then. No one would want to marry her. She'd wind up on the shelf. And what would she do to earn her keep? Who would hire a governess with no references?

"Oh, miss I really don't think you should do this."

The words broke in on Susan's reverie and she looked up, startled, to see a young woman

AN INNOCENT IMPOSTER

had joined her on the wooden bench outside the Golden Cross and was peering at her in concern. "I beg your pardon?" she said.

"It is very dangerous," continued the girl, twisting her cloak nervously. "What if something terrible happened to you? I am sure I would be blamed."

"I am afraid you have me confused with someone else," said Susan.

The girl looked hurt. "Oh, now. There's no need to go play-acting already. Not with me, miss." She lowered her voice. "You've given me very good references, and I do thank you. But I don't wish to be turned off and have to find another mistress. Please, won't you reconsider and take me with you?"

"Harris!"

The sharp voice made the girl jump and turn around, and both she and Susan stared at the female who stood before them. "Miss?" stammered the girl.

"Run along now, Harris," said the other woman. "The stage will be leaving any minute. I shall be fine, I assure you."

The girl sighed in resignation. "Yes, miss," she murmured, and with one last astonished glance at Susan, she melted into the crowd.

"How very amazing," said the newcomer, seating herself on the bench next to Susan. "I almost feel I am looking into a mirror. Of course, your mouth is a little wider than mine. And your hair a little lighter in color, but really the resemblance is most remarkable. Her glance fell on Susan's reticule, an extravagant purchase made when she had thought her position secure. "Even our reticules are alike," the girl observed. "Why, we could be sisters!" She giggled. "Do you think, perhaps, we are?"

Susan didn't know what to think. Wondering if she were experiencing some sort of delirium caused by a worried brain, she blinked and looked again. The girl was still there. Susan shook her head. The resemblance truly was remarkable. "I am sure I would have known if I had a sister," she said as much to herself as the girl.

"One never can tell," said the girl gaily.

"My name is Susan Layne," she offered.

"I am Arabella Leighton," announced Susan's new friend. She lowered her voice. "I am an heiress, and I am running away."

Susan looked at her dubiously. The girl's simple cape and gown were the clothes of the serving class, but her bearing and her extreme self-confidence all bespoke the lady. Of course, the girl could simply be putting on airs. Susan, herself, had played at being the grand lady on occasion and was sure it couldn't be that difficult.

"You don't believe me," accused Miss Leighton.

"Well," hedged Susan.

"Here. I shall prove it," said Miss Leighton. She fished in her reticule and pulled out a calling card and handed it to Susan. "There. You see?"

"Oh, my," said Susan.

"My guardian is an ogre," Miss Leighton confided.

"Does he beat you?" asked Susan breathlessly.

"Well, no," admitted Miss Leighton. "But he is an ogre all the same. He is completely heartless. I am sure he never wished to be my guardian. In fact, I am sure he never thought to be, for who could have known my papa would die so suddenly?"

"Your papa is dead?" stammered Susan.

Miss Leighton shrugged. "It is all water under the bridge now. I have lived with my Aunt Elizabeth for some time, and she is very nice, but Barrymore says she has more hair than wit."

"Barrymore?"

"My guardian. Barrymore is his family name. His title is Earl of Mayfield. He really is a most tiresome man, always lecturing me about not being a hoyden. I may be a hoyden, but he is an ogre. Can you imagine? Forcing a lady to become engaged to some fat old toad before she's barely begun her season?"

"Surely your guardian cannot force you to marry someone you dislike," pointed out Susan.

"He has as much as done so," insisted Miss Leighton. "Aunt Elizabeth said the old toad was such a very good catch, and it did not matter whom I married, for once a lady is married she may have any number of cicisbeos, and she rarely has to be bothered with her husband, anyway. And, of course, Redburrough does have a great fortune, and a fine estate in Hampshire. So, I allowed him to propose. But the more I thought on it, the more I didn't wish to marry him. After all I would as lief marry someone young and handsome, even if he were a wastrel, rather than a man who must wear a corset."

Susan's eyes grew round. "He wears a corset?"

Miss Leighton nodded. "I am sure of it, for whenever he bows over my hand I hear it creak. Barrymore said I shall marry him anyway." Miss Leighton tossed her head. "Well, I shall show Barrymore. I am going to my cousins in Brighton." A wicked smile appeared on Miss Leighton's face. "I should like to be a fly on the wall when he learns I did not go shopping, but instead, have vanished. And I shan't tell him where I am for a good fortnight."

"Gracious!" exclaimed Susan, amazed at such temerity.

A tall man with a plain face and carroty hair had been inspecting the wheels and axles of the coach. Now he straightened and called out, "All those with passage booked on the Eclipse leaving at two o'clock, please come board."

The two young women stood up. "Oh, my," said Miss Leighton. "Look at our driver. Isn't he the most dashing man?"

Susan followed her gaze to see the coachman strutting up to the coach. Followed by a gaggle of admiring boys, he was, indeed, dashing in his multiplicity of coats and his broad-brimmed hat. He was on the hefty side, with a florid complexion and big hands, and reminded Susan of a large ham.

"There was no room inside the coach," said Miss Leighton, "so I booked passage on the top."

"I have heard that can be dangerous," said Susan.

"Stuff," scoffed Miss Leighton. "It will be great fun. I shall tell you all about it when we stop at Croyden."

Susan followed Miss Leighton to the coach. As she squeezed in past a rotund man and a middle-aged woman, she wondered if, perhaps, Miss Leighton had had the right idea. Surely the passengers on the roof breathed cleaner air.

The air in the carriage was musty and tainted by previous passengers. Susan could smell the lingering scent of unwashed bodies, and a faint hint of vomit hung about the interior like an unpleasant prediction.

Ah, well, she thought stoically. At least I am not going so far as Brighton. This was small consolation, however, for Crawley, her destination, was nearly as far.

All the passengers were now ready. The coachman cracked his whip, and the Eclipse made its dramatic exit from the inn yard to the blaring of the horn and the clapping and cheering of the Londoners who had come to view the spectacle.

The rotund man leaned back against the squabs with a lusty sigh. "Well," he announced to the company, "five hours 'til Brighton." He pulled a small silver flask out of his coat and said, "Here's to a safe journey."

He passed it to a gray-haired, bespectacled man seated next to him. The man thanked him and took a swig.

"Here's to an uncomfortable journey, more like," complained the woman seated next to Susan. "Can they not air these coaches better?"

The rotund man shrugged and said, "I suppose anyone who would rather breathe clean air may ride atop the carriage as this young lady's sister has done."

Susan opened her mouth to protest that the girl was no relation, but the woman jumped in before her. "Ha!" she snorted. "Ride on this thing and risk breaking my neck? I think not. Anyone foolish enough to book passage on top of a coach deserves just what they get if you ask me."

They hit a pot hole and the coach gave a bounce. Susan heard a squeal from the roof and then high pitched laughter. Oh, to be

Miss Leighton, wealthy and pampered, running away to cousins in Brighton.

The Eclipse made its first stop in Croyden and the passengers were allowed to disembark and stretch and, if they wished, have something to eat. However, Susan found herself too tired to even think of food. Like herself, the bespectacled man had little interest in food, ordering only tea. However, Susan noticed that the rotund man managed in the short time they were in the dining room to consume steak and kidney pie, oysters, several hot muffins and two tankards of ale.

The middle-aged woman, who had introduced herself as Mrs. Battles, did equal justice to the plate set before her. "You must eat something, dearie, or you'll be right knocked up by the time we reach Brighton."

Susan merely shook her head.

Miss Leighton's appetite seemed not to have suffered, either, and she confessed to Susan as she dabbed at her mouth with her napkin that she had found the brisk breeze most invigorating.

Susan listened as Miss Leighton rhapsodized about travel on top of a coach and thought how very ill disguised her new friend was. In spite of her serving class clothes, she gave herself away each time she spoke. Susan wondered if, put in the kind of lovely clothes Miss Leighton was accustomed to, she would so plainly show her upbringing.

As they left the inn, Susan noticed a group of young men lounging against the inn. They were extremely mirthful, and it didn't take her long to discover the reason for their great mirth lay inside the tankards they held.

One man in particular stood out; perhaps, she decided, because the others seemed to defer to him. He was a picture in his bottle green coat, his buff colored pantaloons and his intricately tied cravat. His curly brimmed beaver perched rakishly over light brown curls and his face, with its snub nose and merry eyes, was boyish and appealing.

He didn't see Susan, for his eye had already been caught by Miss Leighton. Susan watched as he observed Miss Leighton's ascent to the top of the carriage, and saw his appreciative smile when that young lady unknowingly gave him a glimpse of her ankle. He cocked his head and said something *sotto voce* to one of his companions and the man laughed uproariously, spilling his ale.

Susan climbed into the coach just as the man pushed away from the inn and strolled over to it. "Good afternoon, coachman!" she heard him call.

"Hullo, dandy," replied the coachman, tolerant amusement plain in his voice.

"I think the seat next to you needs warming."

"If you thinks you can keep it you can have it for a price," returned the coachman.

Not wanting to appear unladylike, Susan restrained herself from peering out the window, but Mrs. Battles had no such compunction. "Oh, my Lord!" she exclaimed. "The fellow's going to ride up there with our driver. Next he'll be wanting to handle the ribbons, and you know where that will land us? In a ditch somewhere, mark my words."

"Not if I have anything to say about it, madam," said the spectacled man. He leaned his head out the window. "Coachman! Are you going to take this fellow up?" he demanded.

"His blunt is as good as yours," replied the disembodied voice.

The man's face reddened, and he subsided onto the seat, his lips pressed tightly together.

"I don't like this one little bit," continued Mrs. Battles.

"Be glad you ain't sitting on top of the rig," said the rotund man. "I pity any one up there if we should have a mishap."

Arabella Leighton stole a glance at the gentleman as he climbed up on the carriage next to the coachman. He looked back at her and grinned, giving her a glimpse of a fascinating dimple before she demurely lowered her eyes.

He called down to his friends, "I shall meet you in Reigate."

"You'll fall off long before then," shouted one of them. "But don't worry. We'll stop and scrape you off the road."

The young man guffawed at this and settled himself next to the coachman.

"So, dandy," said the coachman. "Are you a nob or do you only dress the part?"

The man swept off his hat to Arabella and gave a half bow. "Sir Richard Gaine, at your service," he said to both Arabella and the coachman.

The coachman leaned over and spat between his teeth onto the road. "And are you one of them Four-in-Hand Club men who drive to Salt Hill and think yourselves to be like real coachmen?"

Sir Richard polished off the remains of his tankard and tossed it away. He hiccoughed, then said, "A gentleman can claim no skill at driving a coach. Is that what you think, coachman?"

The coachman merely shrugged.

"Do you think I cannot handle those ribbons?" demanded the dandy.

"Sober, maybe," replied the coachman.

"Sober, definitely," corrected Sir Richard. "Even drunk, which, I assure you, I'm not. Let me have 'em. I shall show you."

"Show me a crown and I'll let you take the ribbons for the next five miles," said the coachman.

AN INNOCENT IMPOSTER

The young man fished in his waistcoat pocket and produced the desired coin. He winked over his shoulder at Arabella and said, "Now you shall see some fancy driving."

The coachman handed over the reins and whip. With a flourish, Sir Richard threw back his whip hand and the long leather thong snaked out.

A painful yelp and bellow to have a care came from one of the passengers toward the back of the roof.

"Oops," slurred Sir Richard.

Arabella giggled and the coachman said, "No more than five miles. Yer drunk as a lord."

"I am not drunk," insisted Sir Richard. And with that he rose up on the box and cracked the whip over the leader's head. The horses increased their speed, and Sir Richard fell back onto the box with a whoop.

"We'll all be killed," predicted the man seated next to Arabella.

"Oh, pooh!" she scoffed. "We will make Brighton in no time at this rate."

"We will see the gates of heaven at this rate," snapped the man. Looking beyond Arabella, his eyes widened in terror and he let out a cry.

The coachman had also seen the approaching racing curricles and moved to take the reins from Sir Richard.

"I can handle the cattle," said the dandy,

pulling the reins away and causing the horses to turn.

"Give me the reins!" roared the coachman, looking at the oncoming carriages.

"There's room!" insisted Sir Richard. "We'll go between and force 'em into ditches on both sides."

Inside the coach, the passengers rocked violently. The cries from the roof were not lost on them, and they looked at each other, wide eyed. "Lord love us," declared Mrs. Battles, putting a plump hand to her breast. "What can be happening out there?"

The gray-haired man pushed his spectacles up his nose and poked his head out the window. He sat back against the squabs with a white face. "Brace yourselves," he advised. "For we are about to have a terrible accident."

"What! What do you mean, sir?" demanded Mrs. Battles.

Before he could answer, the coach jarred and lurched and seemed to bounce off something. The terrified whinnies of frightened horses mixed with human screams, and Susan braced herself and held her breath as the vehicle careened along on two wheels.

The coach finally landed on its side, and Susan found herself tipped on top of the older woman, with her bonnet in her face and the skirt of her gown halfway up her

AN INNOCENT IMPOSTER

leg. The two men lay opposite them in a tangled, sputtering heap.

"Lord bless us," Mrs. Battles moaned. "I think my arm is broken."

Susan scrambled off the woman as best she could. The door of the carriage was now the ceiling, and through the side windows she could see that what had been blue sky no less than an hour ago was turning gray with the promise of rain. A carriage accident and a rain storm. What more could happen?

Mrs. Battles let out another boisterous moan, and the gray-haired man promised her assistance and tried to disentangle himself from his portly fellow sufferer. As Susan took stock of the condition the other travellers inside the coach, she realized that the passengers on the roof had most likely fared worse than they. "Oh, dear," she gasped. "The people on the roof!"

"Now, don't you worry, young lady," huffed the rotund man encouragingly as he tried to right himself. "I am sure your sister is just fine."

At that moment the weathered face of the coachman appeared in the window. "Well," he said heartily. "Are we all right in here?"

"We certainly are not!" snapped the gray-haired man. "And I can assure you, you will rue the day you took that young jackanapes up onto the box with you, sir!"

The coachman scowled, then disappeared. A moment later the coach door was yanked open and a beefy hand reached in for Susan. "'Ere, now, miss. Give me your hand and I'll pull you out."

He hoisted Susan out of the carriage, and the scene before her made her gasp. People lay scattered about the road like abandoned rag dolls, singing a chorus of moans. Some ten feet behind them, a bright yellow curricle lay upended in a ditch, and a gentleman in a muddied coat was attending to two very skitterish grays. Far in the distance another curricle tooled off, a little rooster-tail of dust chasing it.

The coachman followed Susan's gaze. "Cowardly cur," he growled. "Off 'e goes, gaily as you please and leaves us all to buffle along on our own."

He turned back to the coach to help the other passengers out and Susan tottered off to search for Miss Leighton.

She saw the dandy sitting on the grassy bank, blinking and shaking his head to clear it. Only a few feet from him lay Miss Arabella Leighton, face down and still as death.

Two

Lord Mayfield watched the Surrey countryside roll by his carriage window and scowled. Bah! What a birthday this had turned out to be. Thirty must be an unlucky number for him.

It was bad enough his mother had started dropping hints about setting up his nursery a full two months before the milestone day, but to have to spend that very day chasing an ungrateful chit who didn't appreciate the match he'd made for her, who wanted to attend masked balls, waltz at Almack's without a patroness's permission, and who now had run away. . . . Run away!

Mayfield realized he was mentally ranting and took a deep breath. He supposed in all fairness he couldn't blame Arabella for bolting. In spite of what that feather-headed aunt had said, Redburrough left much to be desired as a suitor. He was richer than Croesus, but he was pushing forty, and he'd lost his figure completely. Too much fine food and not enough exercise, concluded Mayfield with scorn as he braced a foot on the seat opposite him and flexed a well muscled leg.

Still, Arabella should have said something sooner. Fine time to decide she didn't want Redburrough, after she'd flirted with him and encouraged him and everything had been set in motion.

Not for the first time, Mayfield wished old Leighton hadn't done him the honor of entrusting him with the guardianship of his only child.

When Mayfield first met his friend, Sir Ralph Leighton had been a widower who could talk of little else besides his lovely young daughter. He came into a sizeable inheritance after surviving the Peninsular war, and quickly parlayed it into a fortune. Having done this, he died, content that his older sister and the young man who had been his fellow officer and dear friend would watch over the girl.

Responsibility had already settled heavily on Mayfield after his older brother foolishly got himself killed in a duel, and it seemed the new earl had barely inherited the title, the estate, and all its accompanying headaches when he'd fallen heir to the guardianship of Miss Arabella Leighton as well.

If she weren't such a spoiled thing, the earl might have married her himself. He remembered when he'd first seen her. She'd certainly made an impression on him then. She was all dimples and smiles, a young girl,

AN INNOCENT IMPOSTER

holding the promise of womanhood, peeping around the library door at him. Her father had called her into the room and she'd entered with lowered lashes and a vixen's smile.

The next time Mayfield had seen Miss Leighton was at her father's funeral. She'd looked at him through lashes glittering with tears and asked whatever was to become of her. Pitiful, he'd thought. Selfish, he later realized, for Miss Leighton's one concern in life was herself.

The third time he'd been in her company was after she'd been fetched to London. He had procured vouchers for her to Almack's, and escorted her and her aunt there. It seemed he'd no sooner turned his back on the girl than she'd gotten into mischief. Mayfield frowned at the memory of Arabella throwing herself into a chair after he'd taken her from the dance floor.

"You know you should not waltz without permission, dearest," old feather-head had fussed. "The patronesses would be most displeased with you."

The moment Arabella pursed her lips into a very kissable pout, Mayfield had known he'd have every penniless noble in London after her before the week was out.

That was when he had decided Arabella should have her future settled before the season went any farther. That was what had led him to decide to move things along with

Redburrough. And *that* was what led to *the scene*.

While that useless aunt had sat by and wrung her hands, Arabella had informed the earl sweetly that she had decided she didn't fancy Lord Redburrough after all, no matter how rich he was. She should never have allowed poor Aunt Elizabeth to talk her into encouraging the man. She might have led Lord Redburrough into believing she intended to marry him, she admitted, admiring the ruby ring on her finger. But now she realized she could do much better. Perhaps Lord Mayfield would take care of this little matter for her?

Mayfield looked at the ring. "That is part of a set, is it not?"

"The Redburrough Rubies," she murmured. "I shall keep this as a memento. I am sure Lord Redburrough shan't mind, since he still has a tiara and necklace, and earrings as well."

"If you won't have the man you shan't have the ring," said Mayfield.

Arabella snatched her hand behind her back. "I shall," she said. "He gave it to me."

"Fine," Mayfield said calmly. "Keep the ring. And you shall keep Redburrough, too, and not give me any more trouble." Ending the interview, he rose.

Before he could leave the drawing room, Arabella jumped to her feet. "You cannot make me marry him. I shall run away first!"

AN INNOCENT IMPOSTER

And with that she'd run out of the room, her aunt's feeble remonstrances unable to stop her.

Remembering the scene made the earl grind his teeth afresh. "Silly, useless woman," he growled. She'd been completely incapable of watching over Arabella. Well, when the runaway returned she'd find she was no longer going to be under the wing of that old bird. For the first time the earl smiled. He'd like to see the chit try to lead his mother on any merry dances!

The town of Reigate came into view. The coachman had instructions to stop at The Swan. The earl was sure he would catch up with his runaway ward here, and he smiled grimly as he thought of how those pretty golden curls would bounce when he shook some sense into Arabella Leighton. That experience would make a very satisfying birthday present.

Inside The Swan's dining room, Susan and her travelling companions sat around a table, digesting browned mutton and potatoes and discussing the fate of the young woman who had been thrown from the carriage roof.

"Much good a doctor will do," predicted Mrs. Battles, rubbing her shoulder. "With that bump on the head, the poor child will probably never again be in her right mind."

Susan's face turned ash white and the rotund gentleman shook his head at such dramatics. "Nonsense," he said bracingly. "It was a nasty bump, but I am sure the young lady will be right as rain within a fortnight."

"Perhaps," said Mrs. Battles cynically. Her gaze strayed to the curly haired dandy, slumped at a table in the corner. "Well, and that one looks to be finding his conscience. High time, I say. I won't be able to lift my arm for weeks, I am sure."

The gray-haired man took off his spectacles and polished them. "It was very good of him to introduce himself and offer to pay us for any inconvenience or injury we might have suffered. Very good."

"Humph," snorted Mrs. Battles, looking at the card the young man had given her. "Sir Richard Gaine. Sir Richard Pauper, most like. His sort is better at forgetting their debts than paying them."

"He bought our meal," pointed out the gray haired man. " 'Tis a start."

"He could have been buying our coffins," put in the rotund man. "I say it is high time someone put a stop to the practice of letting any young blade with a little gold in his pocket and no sense in his head take the reins of a public conveyance. We were all fortunate no one was killed."

"That poor young woman seems to have fared the worst," said Mrs. Battles. She looked at Susan. "Are you sure you ain't related, dearie?" she asked.

"The resemblance is purely chance," said Susan.

"Amazing," said Mrs. Battles. She sighed and shook her head. "Such terrible news that girl's family has awaiting them. Look, there's the doctor. Do one of you gentlemen go and ask him how the poor child is faring."

The gray-haired man obliged and crossed the room. But Susan noticed that Sir Richard reached him first. She watched as he questioned the doctor, the middle-aged man standing shamelessly next to him, taking in everything. At last Sir Richard fished out a roll of notes from his waistcoat pocket and pressed them into the doctor's hand, shaking it effusively, then vanished from the dining room. The gray-haired man returned to the table.

"Well?" prompted Mrs. Battles.

"The doctor said she has suffered a nasty bump on the head and has badly sprained her left arm, but he predicts she will be right as rain eventually, and said she may possibly even be allowed to leave her bed in a week. The young man has gone up to see her."

"Unchaperoned?" Mrs. Battles was plainly shocked.

"Oh, I am sure the landlord's wife is still with her," put in the man.

"Well," said Mrs. Battles, "I'll just go up and offer my services, I think. Someone should send word to that poor child's family."

Susan watched Mrs. Battles bustle off and

swallowed nervously, knowing whom that someone would have to be. She hated to betray Miss Leighton to her guardian, but really, she could hardly leave the poor girl alone in an inn for an indeterminate amount of time and not let someone know of her whereabouts. If she only had asked the name of the family in Brighton to whom Miss Leighton was going. But all Susan knew was the name of the ogre, and she couldn't bring herself to write him. Perhaps, she concluded, she had best follow Mrs. Battles up to Miss Leighton's room and offer to draft a letter to her family in Brighton for her.

She excused herself to the two men and left the dining room. She got no further than the hallway when a fine-looking, tall gentleman strode through the entrance door and planted himself in front of her. Susan blinked at the vision of virility and power standing before her. Layers of coat, waistcoat and shirt fit snugly over a torso as fine as any Greek statue, and the man's buff colored pantaloons could not hide the fact that he had a strong, muscular leg. His hair, cut in the harsh lines of a Brutus, was the color of coal. His eyes were striking—deep set and intense. His nose was straight and finely chiselled. Even his mouth was pleasing, in spite of the fact that it wasn't smiling. His jaw appeared square, but that, Susan realized, could be simply an illusion, caused by the pugnacious angle at which it was set.

AN INNOCENT IMPOSTER

He swept her with a haughty look. "I trust you have been enjoying yourself," he said, his voice frigid.

"I beg your pardon?" stammered Susan.

"I shan't stand here bandying words with you in a public dining room," snapped the man. "My carriage is outside."

Well! Of all the nerve. "How happy for you," replied Susan haughtily and turned toward the stairs.

In a step the gentleman cut her off. He took her arm in a viselike grip and snapped, "I am done playing this game, Arabella."

Arabella? Oh, dear. Was that not Miss Leighton's Christian name?

"You will accompany me home at once and pray heaven that no one has heard of this escapade," commanded the man. As the stunned Susan showed no immediate signs of obeying, he began to walk her toward the door.

"Stop this at once!" commanded Susan. "Are you mad?"

"You have brought me close to it," said the man. "Now, unless you wish to be in even more trouble than you already are, I suggest you walk with me to the carriage with as much dignity as you can muster. Although from your behavior thus far this season, I realize you have little enough of that," he concluded, his voice acid with scorn.

Susan tried to plant her feet, but the man's strong weight was too much to resist.

"You must stop this minute!" she demanded. "There has been a mistake."

"And you have made it," he said between clenched teeth as he hurried her out the door. Susan tried to resist her captor all the way to the carriage, but the mud gave her no foothold and the wet wind swallowed her protests. A footman jumped to open the carriage door and let down the steps, and Susan quickly found herself propelled into the fine leather interior of a rich man's traveling coach. So much room, some distant part of her noticed as the door shut behind them. And no foul smells.

Never mind that, she told herself sternly. This was obviously Miss Leighton's guardian, the ogre, and she must tell him at once about his ward. But before she could begin, the carriage jerked to life. Panic shot through Susan. "Stop! You must stop the carriage!" she cried.

The earl held up a hand. "Please, Arabella. No more."

"But I am not Arabella!" protested Susan. "I am afraid, sir, I mean, your lordship, that you have mistaken me for someone else."

The aristocratic black eyebrows raised. Gray. The gentleman's eyes were gray. Suddenly he burst into laughter. "Oh, that is rich. I might have known you would brazen it out to the end."

Susan looked at him, perplexed. "You don't believe me?"

"Oh, of course I believe you," he replied,

AN INNOCENT IMPOSTER

his voice heavy with sarcasm. "And who, pray, might you be?"

"I am Miss Susan Layne, and I find your rudeness offensive."

"I do humbly beg your pardon," said the earl, his voice devoid of humility. "Do tell me more of yourself, Miss . . . Layne?"

Susan raised her chin. "I am a governess," she said.

The earl nodded. "I see," he said slowly. "And where have you hidden your charges?" Susan blushed and he continued. "And how is it you come to know who I am?"

"I know you because Miss Leighton told me of you."

"When did she tell you of me?"

"Why, at the Golden Cross," began Susan.

"Really, Arabella, for what sort of simpleton do you take me?" interrupted the earl, scowling.

"Oh, I know it sounds preposterous," said Susan.

"It sounds ridiculous!" he snapped.

"Yes, ridiculous," agreed Susan. "I, myself, was amazed at the resemblance."

"It certainly is remarkable," sneered Woodhaven. "You are quite like Arabella . . . right down to your reticule."

The earl bit off the last words, and Susan was afraid the next thing he might bite off would be her head, but she valiantly persisted. "Here. I can prove my story." She fished in the reticule and produced the calling card Miss Leighton had bestowed on her.

"How amazing," drawled the earl. "A calling card from your very own reticule. Really, Arabella. You make yourself ridiculous, carrying on in this fashion. Are you really so hen-witted as to think that by simply donning your maid's dress and lowering your voice you can fool me into thinking you someone else?" His gaze flicked over her. "You might have planned your disguise more carefully. The cheap gown is wonderful, but the reticule hardly fits. It is as good as an advertisement in the Gazette."

Tears of anger and shame sprang to Susan's eyes. How dare he call her gown cheap! And, oh, why wouldn't he believe her? "If you would but take the time to return inside that inn, you would find the real Miss Leighton abed with a sprained arm," she scolded.

"Ah yes," said the earl in a bored voice. "The carriage accident. I saw the ruined equipage on the road. How fortunate for me, else I would have had to waste my time chasing you farther."

"Heartless, wicked man! Even as you speak your ward is lying on a bed of pain."

The earl cut her off. "I am afraid this originality is belated, my dear. Now. I have heard quite enough tales for one day. I wish to hear no more. You will oblige me by remaining silent until we reach home."

"I shall do nothing of the kind!" declared Susan angrily. "You are kidnapping me against my will."

The earl slouched against the squabs, propped his feet on the seat opposite, shut his eyes and pushed his curly brimmed beaver down over them. "It will do you no good whatsoever to cry and carry on, Arabella. In fact, if you continue to do so I shall turn you over my knee and spank you until you are forced to finish out our journey lying on your belly. So I suggest you admit defeat and be silent."

Susan opened her mouth to protest further, thought the better of it and fell silent. Miss Leighton was right. This man truly was an ogre!

Miss Arabella Leighton lay in a bed in a small but clean room at The Swan and studied the handsome face that peered at her so anxiously. Who was this person? Was he someone she should know? Trying to remember brought fresh pain pounding through her head. She moaned.

"Does it hurt very badly?" asked the young man.

"Yes," she managed. Why? Why did her head hurt? And why was she lying in this bed? "What happened?" she asked.

"You don't remember?"

"Poor lamb," clucked a woman's voice.

Poor lamb? Something truly terrible must have happened to her. Arabella searched her mind for some image from the past. Nothing would come. "No," she said, and tried to lessen the pain in her head by concentrating on the softness of the pillow beneath it.

"There was an accident," said the man. "You were thrown from the carriage. You bumped your head."

Arabella's arm felt funny. Why was it all trussed up?

The man seemed to read her thoughts. "You injured your arm," he informed her.

"It hurts," she announced.

"The doctor has given you laudanum. It won't hurt much longer."

"Who are you?" she asked.

"Sir Richard Gaine, at your service."

"Sir Richard," she murmured. "Should I know you?"

"We have not been formally introduced," admitted Sir Richard. "I would like to know your name."

A dulling fuzziness was creeping across Arabella's throbbing head now. Talking was such an effort. So was thinking. That must be why she could not find a name to give the young man. "Don't know," she sighed, and let her heavy eyelids fall.

Three

It was late when Susan and her escort arrived in London, and the exclusive neighborhood of Mayfair had come to life. Lights blazed from elegant town houses as the Upper Ten Thousand met to eat, dance and generally celebrate the joys of money and position.

If she had not been so upset, Susan would have found the scene passing outside the carriage window fascinating. But her mind was otherwise occupied with trying to think how she could convince the Earl of Mayfield she wasn't his ward. And it was only when the steps were let down that she realized the carriage had stopped and she was in infinitely worse trouble than she'd been in Reigate. She sat staring at the open door while the footman waited to hand her out of the carriage.

"Arabella?" came the earl's voice.

Susan turned wide eyes to him. "Where are we?" she asked.

"You know very well where we are," he snapped.

"Am I to stay with you?" Susan continued nervously.

"You shan't be staying with that totty headed aunt of yours, I can assure you," replied the earl, satisfaction in his voice. "From now until the day you wed Redburrough you will be under the watchful eye of my mother."

"Your mother lives here?"

The earl let out a long sigh. "I ceased playing games on my twelfth birthday. I have no desire to revive the custom for my thirtieth."

"It is your birthday?"

The earl nodded. "And you have given me a present this day such as I shall never forget. Now, do you get down or do I haul you down?"

Susan scurried out of the carriage. From the earl's tone of voice she knew she had best ask no more questions. She only hoped his mother was more reasonable.

A sour-faced butler let them in and they went up a staircase. At the top of the landing, Susan made a guess and turned toward the wrong door. This served to deepen Lord Woodhaven's frown, and he took her arm in a fierce grip and guided her into a room done elegantly in colors of gold and cream.

Susan had only a moment to take in the gold brocade drapes, the feel of thick Aubusson carpet underfoot and the sight of a blazing fire framed in marble before her attention was demanded by the striking woman on the sofa. The woman had hair as black as the earl's, with a whisper of gray, and the same distinctive eyes—the earl's mother, without a doubt. Compared to Susan's mother, who was plump and much more weathered looking, this woman seemed a girl. It was only as Susan drew closer that the telltale signs of aging, the lines around the eyes and the slightly sagging chin, were noticeable. Her face was a mask of cold disapproval. The Ice Queen, thought Susan and her stomach roiled.

"Well, and what have you to say for yourself, young woman?" demanded the countess.

Susan had a great many things to say, none of which Lady Mayfield would believe. She hesitated, unsure how to reply.

"She has had a good deal to say ever since I found her, I assure you," said the earl. He turned a sardonic smile on Susan. "And if you wish, you may be so foolish as to try your story on my mother. I am sure she will find it all vastly amusing. As for myself," here he turned to Lady Mayfield, "I intend to go to Brooks' and enjoy what is left of my birthday."

"Of course," said her ladyship. She rose, linked her arm through his and walked him to the door. She spoke in soft accents, soothing, "I am so sorry your day had to be ruined by this naughty child. I can assure you, Gerard, you shall have no more trouble."

No more trouble? That did not bode well, thought Susan, and bit her lip.

The earl dutifully kissed his mother's cheek, bowed coldly to Susan, and left the room.

The older woman turned to face Susan with a steely look in her eyes. "Now, my dear. Sit down. I am sure you are fagged to death, but before I allow you to find your bed we will have a talk."

Susan sat, grateful to find a chair to hold her up, for her legs had suddenly become incapable of the task.

Lady Mayfield returned to the sofa and sank gracefully onto it. "I am well aware," she said languidly, "that when you were under your aunt's supervision the poor creature danced to whatever tune you piped. I, however, am made of sterner stuff."

Gray eyes hard as marble surveyed Susan, and she could well imagine what a formidable foe this woman might make.

"Your aunt was afraid of scenes," continued her ladyship. "I am not. It would not bother me in the least to box your ears in front of the servants. Nor would I think twice about hauling you from a ballroom floor. Whether or not your gowns are ruined is of no consequence to me, so I should not hesitate to pour punch on you at a rout if you took it into your head to throw a tantrum."

Susan paled as her ladyship listed her

AN INNOCENT IMPOSTER 41

threats in a soft, elegant voice. How would she ever be able to make this woman believe her? And if she couldn't convince Lady Mayfield, what hope had she of making anyone else believe her?

"I trust I make myself clear," said her ladyship, arching a delicate, black eyebrow.

Iron in silk, thought Susan. She nodded.

"Then I am sure we will do famously," said her ladyship, and rewarded Susan with a smile—the smile of a victor to the vanquished.

Susan bowed her head, acknowledging defeat. There must be something she could say to show this woman she wasn't the horrible creature the earl had painted her. "I am sorry to have spoiled his lordship's birthday," she said in a small voice.

"Running away was a childish and stupid thing to do," observed her ladyship.

Susan sighed. "One should always face one's problems," she agreed. "I only wish I knew how to take care of this one," she added in a mutter.

"You take care of it by telling Lord Redburrough you are afraid you mistook your heart, and by returning his ruby ring," said her ladyship tartly. "I see you are not wearing it. I congratulate you on at least having enough sense to leave it off when you were traveling. I trust it is safe?"

Ring? Oh, dear. "Er, yes," stammered Susan.

"Good," said Lady Mayfield briskly. "Now, I suggest we find our beds. It has been an extremely long and tiring day."

Susan sighed. "It certainly has," she agreed.

Lady Mayfield rose and Susan followed suit, hoping her ladyship might inadvertently give her some clue as to the whereabouts of her bedroom. The countess tugged the bellpull. "Childers will show you which room is to be yours," she said, and left Susan standing alone, wondering if she should follow Miss Leighton's example and run away before she could be plunged further into this bumble broth.

Susan had more than enough for coach fare to Crawley. But how she hated to part with it now that she was no longer employed! Yet what else could she do? She could hardly remain here, deceiving an earl and heaven only knew who else.

Too late to run away. The sober visaged Childers was at the door, bowing respectfully, and offering to show her to her room. "Thank you," she murmured, and meekly followed him.

The bedroom in which she was to sleep was larger and grander than anything she'd ever known. Thick velvet curtains hung at the windows and an even thicker carpet cushioned her feet. A huge canopied bed promised sweet dreams, and a roaring fire

AN INNOCENT IMPOSTER 43

in the grate made the room feel cozy and safe.

Tomorrow she would have to find a way to sort out this misunderstanding, but as everyone seemed determined to believe her to be Miss Arabella Leighton, she might as well enjoy the comforts of Miss Leighton's sumptuous life for one night. She would be back to being shabby-genteel Miss Layne soon enough.

The door to the dressing room opened, signaling the approach of Miss Leighton's abigail. For a moment, relief and disappointment swirled in Susan's mind. Of course the lady's maid would know her for the imposter she was and thus be able to help her clear up this misunderstanding. Yet that bed had looked so inviting! But the girl who humbly approached Susan wasn't the girl she had encountered while waiting for the Eclipse. This was someone new. "Where is . . . ?"

The girl ducked her head and curtsied. "She didn't come back, miss. I were . . . was hired to take her place."

"Didn't come back?" echoed Susan. Of course, the girl had mentioned something about Miss Leighton giving her references. She was now employed in some other fashionable house and could not help Susan. *Or betray you,* came a wicked thought. Susan pushed it firmly away. I shan't take advantage of poor Miss Leighton's misfortune, she vowed. First thing in the morning I shall clear up this misunderstanding. "Who are you?" she asked the girl.

"I am Brown, miss."

"Well, Brown. Help me off with my gown," said Susan, trying to sound like Miss Leighton.

"Yes, miss," said the girl, and jumped to do her bidding.

Susan couldn't help but smile. She was actually quite good at being a grand lady. If need arose, she could play this part.

Suitably attired for slumber in a beribboned nightshift much finer than anything she'd ever owned, Susan dismissed her maid, then climbed into the large, soft bed and dismissed all her worries as well. Tomorrow would take care of itself. Tonight she would enjoy the pleasant slumbers of a pampered heiress.

Luxury agreed with Susan, and she slept well, but with morning came the return of conscience. She summoned her abigail, determined go downstairs immediately and clear up the misunderstanding that had brought her to the house of Mayfield.

"What would you like to wear today, miss?" asked Brown eagerly.

Susan realized she had no idea what Miss Leighton had in her wardrobe. If she confessed such a thing the girl would surely think her mad. With sudden inspiration, she said, "You pick a gown for me, Brown."

Brown's eyes widened. "I, miss?"

That had been a misstep. But Susan decided to brazen it out. "Yes. Why not?" she added airily. "I am sure you will find something suitable."

Brown gulped and went nervously to the wardrobe, and Susan was stricken with guilt. Poor girl. She must think this is some sort of test I am giving her.

But Brown managed to rise to the occasion, outfitting her mistress in a willow-green morning gown with puffed sleeves and a bodice embroidered with tiny pink rosebuds. Feeling very much like an imposter, Susan went to find Lady Mayfield and make her confession.

She found her ladyship in her sitting room, reading a copy of Miss Edgworth's *Ormand*. The countess turned her book over in her lap and surveyed Susan.

"I hope I don't disturb you," ventured Susan.

"You do," said her ladyship lightly. "But from what my son tells me, disturbing others has never given you cause for concern."

"I shall leave you to your book," said Susan stiffly and turned to go.

Lady Mayfield smiled at this. "Never mind. You are here now. What do you wish? If it is to go shopping, I can tell you I have no intention of rewarding your scandalous behavior of yesterday with an expedition to Oxford Street."

Susan felt a guilty blush stain her cheeks and had to remind herself that it was not she who had run away. "Your ladyship, I am afraid there has been a grave misunderstanding," she began.

Lady Mayfield raised an eyebrow. "Oh? I thought I had made myself perfectly clear last night."

"You did," said Susan. "But I am afraid there has been a mistake."

A cynical smile stretched the countess's lovely lips. "My but we do step 'round our own culpability, do we not?"

Susan bit her lip. This was going to be even more difficult than she imagined. How to begin? "Has your ladyship, perhaps, ever met a person who bore a strong resemblance to someone else?"

Lady Mayfield shrugged. "Perhaps. I cannot remember at the moment. What has that to do with anything?"

"A great deal, I assure you. Yesterday I met a young woman who looked so very much like myself that her very own abigail mistook me for her."

Lady Mayfield grimaced. "What Banbury tale do you tell me?"

"It is no tale, I assure you. I am afraid your son has mistaken me for his ward. I am not really Arabella Leighton."

"And, pray, who might you be? The Prin-

AN INNOCENT IMPOSTER 47

cess Charlotte? Oh, really, Arabella," continued her ladyship before Susan could speak, "I shall not have my intelligence so insulted. Leave me at once."

"But your ladyship," protested Susan.

"At once," commanded Lady Mayfield, pointing to the door.

Susan sighed and departed. This was most discouraging. She wandered aimlessly down the hall, wondering what she was going to do next.

Mama! Of course. Why had she not thought of it before? She would write to her mother, tell her of her predicament and ask her to come to London. No one could doubt the word of a girl's own mama, and if Susan's vouched for her identity the earl would have to believe her.

Susan hurried to her bedroom and seated herself at the escritoire which sat in the corner. It had considerately been stocked with pen and paper and she grabbed both and began to write.

Dear Mama, I am in terrible trouble. I am afraid I have lost my post, but alas, that is not the worst of it. On my way home to tell you of my misfortune, I was mistaken for an heiress, whose guardian is the Earl of Mayfield. I am currently staying at his house in London. Neither the earl nor his mother will believe I am not his ward, and they are forcing me to remain here. And even worse, they plan to marry me to a Lord Redburrough. Dearest mother, please take the first coach to London and come help your poor Susan. The earl cannot doubt a mother's ability to identify her own daughter, and I fear that is what it will take to free me from this wicked deception which has been forced upon me.

Susan reread her letter, deemed it properly urgent, then signed it, dusted it and put it in an envelope. She would have to ask the earl to frank it, but surely he would be open minded enough to do that.

The earl, she learned, was not yet awake, so she awaited him in the drawing room, pacing before the fireplace. By two o'clock in the afternoon, she had grown tired of the drawing room and was about to venture off in search of the library when Mayfield put in an appearance.

The sight of her obviously did not gladden his heart. He frowned. "Good afternoon, Arabella," he said, his voice clearly lacking in enthusiasm.

"Your lordship, could I have a word with you?" asked Susan.

He sighed. "You are bored. You wish to go calling."

"No!" cried Susan. Seeing the earl's surprised stare, she tried again. "That is, I am sure it is very kind of you to offer . . ."

"I was not offering," said Mayfield.

AN INNOCENT IMPOSTER

Susan digested this and blushed.

"I am waiting, Arabella. What is it you wish?"

She held out the note. "I wish you to frank this, please."

The earl took it and read the envelope. "And who is Mrs. Layne?"

"My mother," replied Susan, trying for a level voice and a calm look.

The earl rolled his eyes. "Really, Arabella. I told you last night . . ."

"It can do no harm to send this letter," interrupted Susan. "If it is all a hum, nothing will come of it. If not, this woman can clear up a grave misunderstanding."

The earl scowled.

"Please," said Susan softly. "I would be so grateful. It is a small thing, after all—surely no great inconvenience to you."

"This a fine time to be worrying about inconveniencing me," retorted Mayfield.

"I shan't ask for anything else," said Susan.

"I have heard those words before," said the earl. "Oh, very well," he added crossly. "Now, go stitch an altar cloth or something and leave me in peace."

"Yes, your lordship," murmured Susan, and made good her escape. She returned to her room and wandered over to the window to look down at the street. Trees and shrubs, elegant houses, sunshine. It was a lovely day for a walk. If she took Brown with her, surely no one could accuse her of trying to run away. And it would be fun to walk the streets of Mayfair as if she lived here. She rang for Brown.

An hour later, attired in a walking gown and a spencer and a bonnet that must have cost Miss Leighton a pretty shilling, Susan was walking down Albermarle Street in the company of her abigail.

A young man tooled by in a curricle. "Good morning, Miss Leighton," he called, removing his hat and bowing with a flourish.

"Good morning," she replied. No sense trying to explain to a stranger driving by that she was not Miss Leighton.

A few minutes later, she encountered two young ladies with a footman in tow, about to enter a landau. At the sight of Susan, they stopped. "Good morning, Miss Leighton," said one. "We did not see you at Miss Morley's ball last night."

What to say? The earl would hardly thank her for explaining that Miss Leighton had been far too busy running away from home the night before to attend a ball. Again, Susan found herself forced to play the part of Miss Leighton. "I am afraid I was indisposed," she said. "I trust you had a wonderful time."

The two women exchanged looks. "Yes, we did," said the same lady who had first spoken.

"I am sure you both looked beautiful and danced every dance," added Susan kindly.

The woman studied her a moment, then said, "Without Miss Leighton there, the gentlemen were forced to pay attention to the lesser beauties."

Susan blushed. "I am sure there are a great many ladies more handsome than I." Two pairs of eyebrows went up and Susan excused herself and walked thoughtfully on. Did Miss Leighton have a reputation for vanity?

"And where do you think you are going?" asked a male voice at her elbow.

Susan jumped and turned to see the Earl of Mayfield falling in step with her. "I was going for a walk," she said. "I am not a prisoner in your house, I trust."

"You have hardly proved yourself worthy of freedom," replied Mayfield.

"Miss Leighton may have proved herself unworthy," Susan corrected him. "Miss Layne, on the other hand, has done nothing."

"Still Miss Layne, is it? And did you introduce yourself to those girls as Miss Layne just now?"

Susan blushed. Somehow, the earl was managing to make her feel guilty for no reason. "No, I did not," she snapped. "I did not think you would like it."

"I certainly would not," agreed the earl. "And I don't care to see you wandering about Mayfair like some cit ogling her betters."

"Well, I am sorry," said Susan irritably, "but I was heartily bored in your house. As my things were left behind at the Swan, I have not even so much as a book of my own to read."

"I have an entire library of books," said the earl. "You had only to ask."

"I did not think you inclined to humor me," said Susan.

"In such matters, I am delighted to humor you," said Mayfield, "although, I must confess, you have not shown much interest in books in the past."

"Miss Leighton may have little interest in books," said Susan, "but I enjoy reading."

The earl smiled a not particularly pleasant smile. "Ah, you are developing your imaginary character quite well," he observed. "Does this Miss Layne harbor bluestocking tendencies?"

"I am not a bluestocking," said Susan coldly.

Mayfield bowed. "I stand corrected. Pray, what sort of books does Miss Layne prefer? Offerings from the Mineva Press, I'll wager."

"I am also fond of Miss Austen, and I read *Queen Mab* with considerable pleasure."

"Shelley. I might have known you would idolize a fellow runaway," scoffed Mayfield.

"I did not say I idolized him," retorted Susan. "But I do enjoy his poetry. At any rate, the aristocracy is riddled with profligates," she added, thinking of one particular profligate who had cost her her position, "so

AN INNOCENT IMPOSTER 53

I don't see why an earl should find Mr. Shelley's behavior particularly shocking."

"I am no profligate," stated the earl.

Susan raised an eyebrow. "Oh? And how did you spend your birthday?"

Mayfield pressed his lips shut.

"Ah, ha," said Susan knowingly.

"My behavior is not on trial here. I am not the one who ran away." Susan opened her mouth to protest, but he didn't allow her time. Instead, he turned her back the direction she had come and said in mocking tones, "Now, if you would be so good as to return with me to the house, I shall endeavor to find something in my library which meets your high standards."

Miss Leighton obviously was not a great reader. What else was she or wasn't she? Susan remembered her encounter with the two young women. Was Miss Leighton as vain as those ladies seemed to think her? "Your lordship, might I ask your opinion of me?" Susan ventured.

"You are spoilt, selfish and headstrong," came the unhesitating reply.

Such brutal honesty took Susan aback. What horrible incidents had occurred to bring the earl and Miss Leighton into such a state of mutual abhorrence? "Oh, my," she managed.

"As you are my ward, it is unnecessary for me to cloak my true feelings," said the earl. "But why you should ask I cannot imagine, for I am sure you have been aware of them for some time."

"Yes," said Susan, more to herself than her companion. "She said you were an ogre."

"Arabella."

The earl's stern tone of voice caused Susan to look up at him in consternation.

"You will cease to speak of yourself as if you were someone else," he commanded. "I will not tolerate it so much as a minute longer."

"But if I am someone else," began Susan.

"You are no one but whom you have always been," the earl informed her. "And if you wish me to believe you someone other than Arabella Leighton, I suggest you behave like someone other than Arabella Leighton."

Susan sighed. "Yes, your lordship," she said meekly. Of course, the earl was right. If she looked so much like Miss Leighton that she even fooled her abigail, how could she hope to convince the earl she was someone else? She would have to wait until Mama arrived or hope to find Miss Leighton's former maid, Harris. Or, here was a possibility she had forgotten; she could bide her time until Miss Leighton's family in Brighton contacted the earl. Then he would see she'd been telling the truth all along.

However, as determined as Lord Mayfield was to disbelieve her, perhaps even that would not convince him, Susan realized. If

AN INNOCENT IMPOSTER 55

Diogenes himself were to present her as the most honest woman in the world the earl would call him a liar.

Diogenes. Susan smiled, realizing any reference to the ancient Greek who had searched so diligently for an honest man would be considered shockingly bluestocking by the earl.

"Have I said something particularly amusing?" he demanded.

"You have said nothing either amusing or kind," Susan replied. "I am afraid my mind wandered."

"Bah," said the earl in disgust. "Why I am even speaking with you I cannot imagine."

"Nor can I," retorted Susan, then felt a sudden wild urge to giggle. Really, this entire situation was utterly ridiculous when one stopped and thought about it. Here she was, a simple governess, insisting she was just that, while everyone around her insisted she was an heiress. And rather a beastly heiress, too. Perhaps it would be fun to see if, posing as Miss Leighton, she could win Lord Mayfield's respect. She might even be able to rid Miss Leighton of her unwanted suitor. Susan had often watched Lady Wight's guests and wondered what it would be like to be in their fine slippers. Well, now fate had presented her with the opportunity to find out first hand. She stole a glance at the earl. He was staring straight ahead, frowning. "Your lordship has still not told me," she said softly, "am I a prisoner in your home?"

"Only if you wish to consider yourself such," said the earl stiffly.

"That is no real answer," pointed out Susan.

"Then let me say that you will be under my watchful eye until Redburrough returns to town and we announce your betrothal in the *Gazette*."

Susan sighed. Ah well, she thought, the earl's house is a very lovely prison. There were certainly worse fates. She smiled at Lord Mayfield in what she hoped was a conciliatory manner. "I am sorry you have been so vexed in the past, but I think I can safely assure your lordship that I am now a new woman."

The earl looked at her suspiciously and she let loose the giggle that had been clamoring to get out, then boldly took his arm. If she was going to play the grand lady, she might as well enjoy it. Someday she would tell her grandchildren of the time she walked down Albermarle street, her hand on the arm of an earl.

They returned inside the townhouse and, true to his promise, Mayfield took Susan into the library. "I think there are enough books here to satisfy the bluest of stockings," he said. "However, I am afraid you will search in vain for *Mysteries of Udolpho*."

Susan had been closely inspecting the shelves as he spoke. Now she took down Miss Austen's *Emma*. "I saw this in Lady Wight's library, but never felt free to ask to read it," she said excitedly, opening the book to peek at the first page.

"Lady Wight's library?" repeated Mayfield.

Susan gave the earl a defiant look and closed the book with a snap.

"Ah, of course, that would be your mistress."

"If your lordship will excuse me?" Susan made to walk past him, but he stepped in front of her, stopping her.

"Why aren't you calling me Barrymore in that irritatingly familiar way you have?" he demanded.

"I don't wish to be irritatingly familiar," said Susan. She moved to step around him.

He countered it with a move of his own. "If you are a governess, why were you alone on the stage for Brighton?" he demanded.

Susan's face flamed.

"Ha!" crowed Mayfield. "I have caught you without an answer."

"If you must know," retorted Susan. "I was dismissed. Without references," she added bitterly.

A wicked smile grew on the earl's face. "Dismissed without references, eh?" He tapped his chin thoughtfully. "Now, why would a governess be dismissed without references, I wonder. Did you beat the children?"

"Certainly not!" gasped Susan.

The earl moved closer to her. "Then there

is only one other reason a governess could be dismissed without references." Susan took a step backward and he followed her. She took another step and found herself backed against a bookcase. The earl planted a hand on either side of her. "If my memory serves me correctly, Lady Wight has a young cub who's been sent down from Oxford, does she not?"

Unable to dissemble, Susan merely looked over the earl's shoulder. "I am sure it pleases your lordship to make light of me," she said stiffly, trying to ignore the frantic pounding of her heart and the heady scent of Hungary Water teasing her senses.

"Do you know what happens to young ladies who tell lies?" whispered the earl. "It is the same thing that happens to naughty governesses."

"Perhaps I should remind you that this is hardly the proper way for a guardian to behave toward his ward," said Susan in a trembling voice.

Mayfield grinned. "Ah, but you are not my ward, remember? You have been telling me so ever since I found you at The Swan."

"If you kiss me I shall scream," threatened Susan, terrified as much by her own wild feelings as the earl's behavior.

"I am told I have such a strong effect on the ladies," said the earl sweetly. "Most of them simply swoon." His face moved threateningly, temptingly closer to hers. "Come

AN INNOCENT IMPOSTER

now, Arabella. Give up the charade. It is most ridiculous."

"Ridiculous is precisely what you are going to feel when you discover I have been telling you the truth all along," scolded Susan. She dipped under Mayfield's arm and ran from the room as if for her life, the sound of his laughter following, stinging her like an insult.

Four

Susan threw her book on the bed. After what just occurred in the library, it would be impossible to concentrate on the adventures of Emma and Mr. Knightly. Their story was dull in comparison to hers. She surveyed herself in the looking glass. She did look pretty in Miss Leighton's gown.

Susan's glance strayed to the wardrobe. What other wonderful gowns did Miss Leighton possess? It would be most impolite to snoop. Susan bit her lip and regarded the wardrobe. She really should know what gowns were available to her.

She went to it and opened the door on a rainbow of muslin and silk. "Oh, my," she breathed and pulled out an evening gown of rose colored silk. She fingered the soft material, then lifted out the gown and went back to the looking glass. She held the dress up to her and smiled at what she saw. The pink turned her complexion to roses and cream.

A knock on her door made her give a guilty start. She ran and shoved the gown back in the wardrobe, then went to answer the door. There stood Arnold, the footman. He looked surprised to see Arabella at the door and not her maid, but he managed to deliver his message all the same. The earl wished to remind Miss Leighton that they would be attending the opera after dinner that evening.

"Please thank his lordship for informing me," said Susan. The footman left to do her bidding and she ran back to the wardrobe and pulled out the rose silk gown. This would do very nicely. Going to the opera in an expensive evening gown. With an earl. Susan felt very much like Cinderella.

She wasn't Cinderella, her conscience reminded her. She was an imposter. But an innocent one, she argued. And surely, so long as she continued to try and make the earl understand the truth of her situation she needn't feel so very badly about wearing beautiful gowns and attending the opera.

"Which gown do you wish to wear tonight, miss?" asked Brown that afternoon as she applied a complexion-wash to her mistress's face.

"I think I shall wear the rose colored silk," said Susan, feeling very much a lady of leisure.

Don't get too accustomed to this, she warned herself. For you will soon be discovered and it will all come to an end.

"And the pink beaded, slippers?" asked Brown eagerly.

"I think so," agreed Susan, pretending she knew to which slippers the maid referred.

Brown nodded excitedly. "And I know just the thing for your hair, if you will allow me to try something new, miss."

Susan smiled. In the face of such enthusiasm, how could she not?

Her new maid was anxious to please and it seemed to Susan that the girl fussed for hours over her clothes and with her hair. But when she finally regarded herself in the looking glass before going down to dinner she realized that Brown was an artist. "Oh, my," she said, turning her head. "This is quite the most elegant hairstyle I have ever had."

Brown turned pink and smiled. "Do you like the little pink rose over your ear, Miss Leighton?" she asked eagerly.

"It is lovely," said Susan. "I am sure every lady I meet tonight will want to know the name of my hairdresser."

"Oh, miss," said Brown, blushing and looking at the floor.

"And now I suppose I should go down to dinner," said Susan. "It would never do to be late to my first dinner with the earl." Her abigail's brows knit and Susan realized she had blundered. She corrected herself. "That is, my first dinner since . . ." Oh, dear. Where was *that* leading? "I'd best be getting

AN INNOCENT IMPOSTER

downstairs," she finished lamely, and explained away her reluctance to reveal to the girl who she really was as a noble effort to protect Miss Leighton's reputation. Pride didn't enter into it at all, she assured herself. After all, she had no need to be embarrassed for who she was or the fact that she was living another woman's life. Neither situation was of her choosing.

The earl and his mother were already in the drawing room when Susan entered. At the sight of her, Lord Mayfield began to smile. But as if remembering who she was, he stopped it from completely forming, leaving only a smirk. "You look lovely tonight, Arabella," he said grudgingly.

"Thank you," she said, trying not to take offense at the earl's behavior. "I am very much looking forward to the opera tonight," she added. "What are we going to see?"

This was obviously the wrong thing to say. The earl frowned. "You know very well we are going to see Catalani sing *Semiramide* at King's Theatre. I have had tickets for the last two weeks."

"Catalani," repeated Susan. "I have heard of her."

"You have heard her," corrected the earl. At that moment Childers appeared to announce that dinner was served, and as they went into the dining room the earl informed his ward that he did not wish to play any of her games this evening.

Susan clamped her lips shut on the retort that begged to escape, determined not to quarrel with him and spoil her Cinderella evening.

She did, indeed, feel like Cinderella when they entered the King's Theatre, also known as the Royal Italian Opera House. She looked with awe over the five tiers of boxes and the gallery that sat over three thousand people and marvelled that she, Susan Layne, governess, should be among this number, and not in the gallery but in the boxes that sat the privileged and wealthy.

"Arabella, do stop gawking," commanded Lady Mayfield. "You make yourself look ridiculous."

"I am sorry," said Susan humbly as she tried to look like a young lady accustomed to sitting in a box at the opera, attempting to imitate the other ladies and gentlemen who were scanning the crowd in a casual manner to see who was and wasn't present. Of course, as she knew no one, this did her little good. "Who is that woman in the box opposite us?" she asked Lady Mayfield, indicating a formidable looking older woman.

"You will not insult my intelligence by pretending you don't know Lady Melbourne," said her ladyship in stern tones. "Nor by feigning ignorance of her daughter-in-law, Lady Caroline Lamb."

Susan looked at the young woman with the

close cropped hair and the heart shaped face and said, "She is quite lovely."

"So you are capable of acknowledging beauty in others," said her ladyship.

"I would hope that I am not such a selfish creature as to be incapable of appreciating beauty in another female."

"Would you?" replied her ladyship thoughtfully.

Hearing the tone of Lady Mayfield's voice, Susan took hope. Perhaps she might yet convince someone in the earl's establishment that she was not Arabella Leighton, spoiled heiress.

Susan returned her attention to the other boxes and caught sight of a familiar family. The man had a neck like an ox and a barrel chest. The woman next to him had fading yellow hair. Her scrawny arms and neck made the generous roundness inside the bodice of her gown look suspiciously like padding. Next to her sat an equally skinny young man with short-cropped, light brown hair.

Susan quickly turned her gaze away, but not before the darling son of her former employer Lady Wight, the Honorable Andrew Caine, rakehell in training, caught sight of her, his eyes rounding in surprise.

Susan plied her fan vigorously and Lady Mayfield asked, "Are you feeling well, Arabella?"

"I am just a little warm," said Susan. "I am sure I shall be fine presently."

The opera began, but Susan saw nothing on the stage. Instead, she saw the pimply-faced youth who had catapulted her into this adventure coming to visit her in Lord Mayfield's box and ending her charade. Of course, she reminded herself, that was her wish. But she had no desire to end it so ignominiously, with the horrible Andrew making sheeps eyes at her and causing her to look like the scheming governess his mama had thought her. As soon as the curtain goes down I shall tell the earl I am feeling the need to stretch, she decided. And I shall stay away from the box until the curtain has gone up again.

But when intermission came, Lord Mayfield forestalled her departure by saying, "I suppose we shall now be bombarded by all manner of fops coming to throw limp compliments at your feet, Arabella."

"Oh, I am sure there can be no one coming to see me," Susan protested. "Perhaps we might walk about a little." She looked nervously to the Wights' box and her heart sunk. Only Lady Wight and her husband remained in it. "I should very much like to stretch," she added.

Too late. A familiar voice was already asking permission to have a word with the lovely lady in the box. "I am Mr. Andrew Caine, son of Lord and Lady Wight," said the voice,

AN INNOCENT IMPOSTER

and Susan's heart fell clear down to the toes of her pink beaded slippers.

"Lord and Lady Wight's son," said the earl in a voice that told Susan he expected to gain great entertainment from this visit. "Do come and sit with us. Arabella, here is an acquaintance of yours come to pay us a visit."

The earl's tone was mocking. Quickly, Susan weighed the shame of being the rich Arabella caught in a fairy tale against looking like a governess with no principles masquerading as an heiress. One final thought tipped the scales. How could she explain to the pesky Andrew why she was with the Earl of Mayfield without bringing shame on the real Arabella? "Miss Lay—" began the young man, and she finished the name for him, saying firmly, "Leighton. I am Arabella Leighton. Have we met?"

He looked at her, puzzled. His eyes slid to Lord Mayfield, who was looking on with interest as a knowing smile grew on his face. "Miss Leighton," he said, and took the proffered hand and bowed over it. "Yes, we have, although it would appear you have forgotten," he added, giving emphasis to his last words. He seated himself next to her, giving her a fine close view of his pimply face. "You are looking more beautiful than ever," he said.

"Thank you," replied Susan primly and wished he would take himself off.

The young man sneaked another look in Mayfield's direction, and seeing the earl's gaze had momentarily shifted from them, lowered his voice and said, "My dear Miss Layne. What a surprise to find you here."

"I am afraid you have me mistaken with someone else," said Susan, trying to will away the blush invading her cheeks.

Mr. Caine looked from her to Lord Mayfield, who was looking like the picture of male curiosity, head cocked to the side and straining to hear. "Ah, so that is how it is," said the youth slowly. He leaned close to her and whispered, "A new start, eh? I'd have kept you as well as Mayfield."

The delicate pink on Susan's face darkened to rose red and she turned in her seat with her back to the future Earl of Wight, fuming and wishing she could rap him on the nose with her fan.

"It would appear Miss Leighton is not feeling quite up to conversing," Lady Mayfield said to him. "It was very kind of you to pay your respects."

"Of course," stammered the young man and made his exit.

"Most interesting," murmured the earl.

Most interesting, Susan repeated miserably to herself. What did that comment mean? She was very much afraid that before the evening was over she would find out.

The earl and his mother discussed Madam Catalani's performance most of the way

AN INNOCENT IMPOSTER

home, and Susan took heart. It would appear his lordship was not going to bring up the subject of Susan's visitor or the fact that she had claimed to be his ward. Her galloping heart settled down to a more sedate pace.

But once they were inside, Mayfield turned to his mother and said, "If you would excuse us, Mother, I wish to speak with Arabella alone."

"Certainly," said her ladyship.

The earl turned to Susan. "Please be so good as to join me in my study."

Susan's heart burst into a gallop again and with leaden feet she walked past him into the study and headed for the fireplace at the far end of the room.

She heard the door shut behind her, but refused to turn around, looking instead at the dying embers on the hearth.

"Did I hear you tell that young man your name was Arabella Leighton?"

"It seemed best," said Susan stiffly.

"It seemed best to tell the truth?" mocked the earl.

"It was not the truth," insisted Susan. "But I had rather have that odious boy think me someone else than to insinuate . . ." Susan stopped herself, letting the sentence hang unfinished.

The earl looked at her sharply. "Insinuate what?"

"Never mind," said Susan. "It is not important."

The earl came to stand behind her. "Before embroiling one of your admirers in this little charade, Arabella, you should have coached him better."

Susan whirled on him. "I am not Arabella! I am Susan Layne. I very much like being Susan Layne, and your calling me by another name does not make me any less Susan Layne. Now, if you wish me to pretend to be your ward I shall continue to do so until we can straighten out this tangle, but I shan't . . . cannot in good conscience pretend to you to be anything other than what I am."

The earl threw up his arms and paced away from her. Looking heavenward, he demanded, "What crime have I committed that I am forced to suffer such punishment?"

"Other than kidnapping?" asked Susan.

"Silence!" commanded the earl. He stalked back to Susan and, shaking a finger in her face, said, "I'll have no more, I tell you. Tomorrow you are at home to visitors. If you so much as mention the name Susan Layne I shall personally rip out your tongue!"

"I did not betray your ward tonight and I shan't tomorrow, either," retorted Susan. "Though why I should allow myself to be a martyr to this family's collected stupidity—"

"Enough!" roared Mayfield. For a moment, he looked as if he would say more, but at last he turned and stomped to the door. "Good night!" he bellered over his shoulder, and slammed it behind him.

"Good night to you, too," growled Susan. She paced the room for a moment, then vented her fury by kicking the earl's desk, which gave her no satisfaction, only a sore toe. This made her all the more angry, and crying, she hopped to the nearest chair and fell into it to rub her throbbing foot.

What an obstinate man! she fumed. What a fool he would feel when he learned the truth. She hoped her mama would come to London soon, for not only her fate hung in the balance, but Miss Leighton's as well.

Miss Leighton! Of course. There lay the answer to all Susan's problems.

Five

Susan went straight to her room and wrote a letter to Miss Arabella Leighton, explaining the great confusion that had resulted from their meeting on the road.

"I assure you, Miss Leighton, I can understand how you might feel reluctant to return to London, but it is most necessary. I have no wish to gain your fortune, but your guardian seems determined to force it upon me, for he cannot imagine me to be anyone other than you, his ward. Please come to London as soon as you are physically able."

Susan felt better after having written this letter, knowing that either this strategy or the arrival of her mother would clear up all misunderstandings. And that pleasant thought sent her into the sound sleep of the innocent.

The following morning she encountered Lord Mayfield in the hallway by the front door. "Perhaps your lordship would be so good as to frank a letter for me," she said, holding out the missive.

AN INNOCENT IMPOSTER

Mayfield looked at her suspiciously, but took it. On seeing the direction on it, his brows lowered and his voice raised. "Arabella!"

Susan quailed before him, sure he was growing taller by the second as he took in breath to berate her.

"Gerard!" Both Lord Mayfield and Susan turned to see the countess coming down the stairs. "Why on earth are you bellowing like a lion with a thorn in his paw? And why are you doing so in the hall where the servants may hear you?"

"It is my fault," said Susan with a sigh. "I wished him to frank another letter for me."

Her ladyship had reached the bottom of the stairs by now. She held out her hand for the letter. "This does not seem such an unreasonable request," she said, as her son handed it over. She looked at the direction and her eyes widened. "What nonsense is this?" she demanded of Susan.

"Someone should inform poor Miss Leighton what has happened," said Susan. "I have no desire to wear another woman's slippers, especially those of an heiress, while she may be suffering great pain and heaven knows what indignities back at The Swan."

"That is very kind of you," said the earl sarcastically.

"Oh, Gerard, honestly," snapped her ladyship. "Send the silly thing. I am sure it is of no consequence to you."

"It is the idea, Mother," protested Mayfield. "To humor her so, when she is, after all, only sending a letter to herself."

"If that is the case, then all we will get in reply is a note from the landlord saying there is no such person staying at The Swan," said her ladyship reasonably. "And the farce will be done." She turned to Susan. "Meanwhile, Arabella, you will kindly remain yourself."

"You mean you wish me to continue to pretend to be Arabella," corrected Susan.

"You know exactly what I mean, young woman," said Lady Mayfield sternly, "and I'll have no more impertinence from you."

"Yes, your ladyship," said Susan meekly.

"Now. Have you breakfasted?" asked her ladyship.

"No," said Susan.

"I suggest you do so, then put on something suitable for callers. We are at home today."

"Yes, your ladyship," murmured Susan, and made her escape.

"You are amazingly good at handling her, Mother," said the earl after Susan had gone into the dining room.

"It is not so very difficult, Gerard."

"Ha!" said Mayfield.

"You make the mistake of letting her see

how much she nettles you. It only encourages her to think of more pranks."

"If she plays many more I shall turn her over my knee." The earl regarded the letter in his hand. "Should I really bother to send this or burn it on the fire?"

"By all means, take the challenge and send it," said her ladyship.

Susan felt the countess's eyes on her that afternoon as they entertained a steady stream of callers. She knew none of the women who passed through the Mayfield drawing room, but it didn't matter, for each woman who called believed her to be Arabella Leighton, and chatted with her accordingly, making it easy for her to maintain the deception that fate had forced upon her.

Their last callers proved to be the young lady Susan had spoken with the day she'd ventured out for a walk and the girl's mama. Miss Amanda Thibble was unremarkable in looks, but it became quickly apparent to Susan that Miss Thibble's mother thought her handsome enough to capture the attention of the Earl of Mayfield. "We had thought we might see your son about today," said the Honorable Mrs. Thibble, trying for a casual air.

"I am afraid he had some duties which called him away from the house," said Lady Mayfield.

"Such a handsome young man," observed Mrs. Thibble. "And so considerate. Amanda was quite flattered that he would ask her to dance a waltz at Miss Morley's comeout."

"I am sure it was his pleasure," said the earl's mama politely. Miss Thibble smiled and blushed and looked at her lap.

Poor Miss Thibble, thought Susan. She fancies the earl. Well, and was that so hard to imagine? He was terribly handsome with that dark hair and those arresting eyes. Obviously, he could, on occasion, make himself agreeable. The Thibble ladies certainly found him so. How, Susan wondered, would he treat her if he didn't believe her to be Arabella?

"Miss Leighton?" came Miss Thibble's voice.

Susan gave a start. "Oh, I beg your pardon," she said. "What were you saying?"

"I only asked if you are looking forward to attending Lord and Lady Allistair's ball," said Miss Thibble in the stiff tones of one who is well aware she is being snubbed.

"Yes, I am," replied Susan.

"I suppose you have every dance promised already," ventured Miss Thibble, her voice tinted with jealousy.

"Oh, no," replied Susan, then wondered what she could say to encourage this poor girl, who was obviously aware of her own inadequacies.

Actually, Miss Thibble was not so very bad

looking. Her face was rather long, but an attractive hairstyle could hide that. Her skin was another matter. It was on the sallow side, and the yellow gown she was wearing seemed to emphasize the fact rather than hide it. The gown did nothing for her hair, either, which was an unremarkable brown. Susan remembered with sudden distaste the pea green pelisse Miss Thibble had been wearing when she'd first encountered her. That had done nothing for the girl, either. Obviously, neither Miss Thibble or her mama had an eye for color.

"I suppose," said Susan thoughtfully, "you have a lovely gown all picked out for the ball."

Miss Thibble seemed surprised by this remark. "Why, yes, I do," she said. "It has a yellow satin slip—"

"Um, hmmm," said Susan slowly, nodding.

Miss Thibble frowned. "Why did you say 'um, hmm' in that manner?"

"I do beg your pardon," said Susan. "I was only thinking how very lovely you would look wearing a gown of willow-green or blue."

"I do have an ice blue gown which is to be delivered tomorrow," said Miss Thibble thoughtfully. "Mama, should I wear my new blue gown to the Allistairs' ball?"

Mrs. Thibble paused in mid-sentence.

"Miss Leighton suggests I would look well in a blue gown."

Mrs. Thibble regarded Susan thoughtfully, then looked at her daughter. "I think I must agree with Miss Leighton," she said. "I am not at all sure that yellow satin one looks well on you, Amanda."

"I think she would look very lovely in blue," ventured Susan.

Mrs. Thibble nodded. "Yes, I must say I agree. Well, it is fortunate we are having one made up in just that color. Now, aren't you glad your mama insisted? Mothers do know best, after all."

Miss Thibble nodded and smiled shyly at Susan. "Miss Leighton always looks so very nice," she said. "I am sure I would be foolish not to follow any advice she may be kind enough to offer."

"That was very gracious of you to advise Miss Thibble," said Lady Mayfield after mother and daughter had left.

"I think she has not much eye for color," said Susan.

"Her mama could make more of her," said her ladyship.

"Most definitely," agreed Susan.

The two women sat awhile longer, discussing their various callers, and when Lady Mayfield left Susan she wore a thoughtful expression.

That night at Lady Belding's rout, Susan caught the countess watching her several times and wondered why her ladyship was observing her so carefully. The smile Lady

AN INNOCENT IMPOSTER 79

Mayfield gave Susan whenever their eyes met was almost as disconcerting as her scrutiny. It was a far cry from the cold look Susan had received on their first meeting, and she couldn't help wondering what thoughts lay behind it.

The next morning Lady Mayfield's son learned what had prompted his mother's sudden inclination toward tolerance. She joined him in the library and lost no time in voicing her opinion. "I begin to think you have misjudged Arabella," she said.

Mayfield raised a skeptical eyebrow. "Oh?"

"The girl is nothing like you described to me," said her ladyship. "Other than insisting on this foolish story, I find her rather sweet. She was most kind to Miss Thibble yesterday, and even went so far as to offer her some much needed advice on what colors she should wear."

"I cannot imagine Arabella assisting another female with anything," said the earl.

"It would appear the child is not so awful as you imagined," suggested his mother.

"She is, believe me. There is still the little matter of a ruby ring."

"Perhaps she means to have Redburrough after all," said her ladyship. "I observed her carefully last night. She is not a flirt."

"Ha!" snorted Mayfield. "Now I know we are not speaking of the same female."

Lady Mayfield sat thoughtful for a moment. "Gerard. Is it possible that you did, indeed, mistake another young lady for Arabella?"

The earl looked at his mother as if she had run mad. "I cannot believe what I am hearing."

Her ladyship shrugged. "I have dealt with a great many young ladies in my time, a great many Arabellas, in fact. And that is why this one bothers me. Other than her stubborn insistence on this wild story, I find her to be a nice girl."

"She is merely trying to turn you up sweet," said Mayfield. "The moment she thinks she has you fooled she'll be off, running away with a fortune hunter or doing something else equally disastrous."

The countess smiled at this. "That will be no easy task, I assure you."

"She managed successfully once before," pointed out Mayfield.

"That was when she had her maid to help her," said her ladyship.

"She has a new maid now."

"Who is in my employ, and who will report to me any and all suspicious behavior," said Lady Mayfield.

This announcement produced a shocked look followed by a bark of laughter. "Mother, Mother," said the earl. "It is a pity women cannot be generals. Wellington could have used your services."

His mother acknowledged his compliment with a bow of the head. "Bearing in mind what you have just said, I suggest you follow the advice I am about to give you."

"And what is that?" asked Mayfield suspiciously.

"Plan to take our guest for a drive in the park this afternoon."

"Guest. Bah," he said, but he did as he was told, and that afternoon Susan sat in his lordship's curricle as they dawdled through the throng of elegant equipages congregating at Hyde Park for the fashionable five o'clock promenade.

Susan had been amazed when the earl invited her to go for a drive. Of course, his invitation had lacked grace. He had merely informed her that she could use some fresh air and to be ready to leave the house at four-thirty. But still, he had offered, and now she looked with awe at the richly dressed people parading along the walkways and sitting in phaetons, twirling parasols. The park was a beautiful sight, a little bit of country right in the heart of London, and Susan looked at its lushness and felt a twinge of homesickness.

"There is Miss Willowby," said the earl, tipping his hat to a young lady seated in a curricle next to a dandy with excessively high shirtpoints and waving frantically. "Do acknowledge her before she tips herself out of Wendell's curricle."

Susan gave a start then did as she was told.

"Really, Arabella," said Mayfield, "I wish you would pay attention. What has you so distracted?"

"I am sorry," said Susan. "It is just that I have never . . ." She caught herself before saying she'd never been in Hyde Park before, realizing that such a statement would only anger the earl. "Seen the flowers looking quite so lovely."

"I didn't think you the sort to be interested in flowers," observed the earl. "Or is that something Miss Layne appreciates?"

"I enjoy flowers," said Susan, refusing to rise to the bait. "There is so much beauty in the world, if we but choose to see it. At least, that is what my mother always says."

"Your mother is dead," said the earl dampingly.

"My mother is alive and well."

The earl's jaw began working and Susan laid a hand on his arm. "It is such a lovely day. Please don't let's spoil it by quarreling. Tell me of yourself."

"You know all about me," said the earl shortly.

"I should like to know more," said Susan, struggling to keep her voice light.

"I cannot imagine what you would wish to know," he said.

"Oh, little things, such as your favorite color."

AN INNOCENT IMPOSTER

The earl rolled his eyes.

"I can guess what it is," offered Susan, determined to bring about a friendly conversation. "Red. That is a strong color, and you appear to be a strong man, a man of action." She looked at him. He nodded curtly, and she pretended to herself that he had smiled. "My favorite color is—"

"Black, I'll wager," he inserted. "The color of night, the color of magic. And deception."

"I am afraid of the dark," said Susan, then added firmly. "I like blue. It reminds me of summer skies." She looked up. "Or spring ones, like this. Those clouds." She pointed to the bits of white floating in the sky. "They look like my grandmother's hair when she is not wearing her wig."

Mayfield made a face. "Please, Arabella. I may have to drive you about the park, but surely my responsibility does not extend so far as to force me to listen to such silly drivel."

"I was merely trying to make polite conversation," said Susan stiffly. "Which is more than I can say for some."

"Ah, that is more like the Arabella I've come to know and detest," said the earl sweetly.

Susan sighed. "That poor girl. No wonder she ran away if this is how you treated her."

"Oh, no. That won't wash. It was you who

planted this animosity between us," said Mayfield.

"Then might I suggest that you allow me to pull it out?" retorted Susan, trying for a calm voice. "Or are you the sort of man who must constantly go digging up past grudges like a dog looking for a bone?"

"I certainly am not!" declared Mayfield.

"I am heartily glad to hear it," said Susan. "For such a trait is most unbecoming in a person, and very uncharitable. After all, people do change."

"And have you changed, Arabella?"

Arabella! How sick she was of that name and all that went with it. "I am a different woman," she said. "And I would be grateful if you would give me an opportunity to prove it."

"I should like to see you try," said the earl.

"Would you?" she asked, her voice a challenge.

Mayfield sighed. "I will give you a chance."

"That is all I ask," said Susan.

The earl said nothing more, and Susan found herself suddenly at a loss for conversational tidbits. After a few minutes, he turned his curricle toward home. It was a silent ride, the silence broken only by Susan thanking Mayfield for taking her driving when they pulled to a stop in front of his house.

"It was my pleasure," he said, and hopped down from the curricle before she could decide whether his words had been sincere or sarcastic.

When he came around to help her down, she could tell by his sober expression that he had not meant what he said, and sighed inwardly. What would it be like to meet the earl without daggers drawn?

Once inside, Susan went to her room and Lord Mayfield went in search of his mother. He found her in her sitting room, reading.

"Well?" she said. "And did you two manage to declare a truce?"

"She assured me she is a different woman," said Mayfield.

"Different, as in changed, or different meaning someone else completely?"

The earl shrugged. "Who can know? With Arabella it is hard to tell exactly what she may mean." He shook his head. "All that drivel about clouds and favorite colors." He sighed and collapsed onto a chair.

"Gerard, what on earth are you talking about?" demanded his exasperated mama.

Mayfield shook his head. "Nothing, only some nonsensical conversation she insisted on having."

"Perhaps she was trying to make a new start."

"If she wishes to make a new start she

may tell me whether she means to have Redburrough or not, and if not what she has done with that ring," said Mayfield. "I should have gotten it out of her this afternoon," he muttered, "but she managed to distract me." He shook his head and gave a grudging chuckle. "Her grandmother's wig, indeed."

Lady Mayfield brought him back to the subject. "Did she seem the same girl to you?"

Mayfield threw up a hand and let it fall limply back onto his lap. "How can I tell? She was pleasant enough. But then, no one was thwarting her."

"Time will tell us the truth, I suppose," said her ladyship with a shrug and picked up her book.

Her son took the hint and left.

The following day Susan had a caller, a young man with a pleasant round face and the hard muscled body of a Corinthian. Mr. Morriville was admitted into the drawing room and mischievous brown eyes danced at the sight of Susan. He bowed politely over Lady Mayfield's hand, then headed for Susan with all the determination of a man about to give chase to a fox. As he bowed over her hand, he smiled at her in what she was sure was a conspiratorial manner. "I called to see if you ladies attend Lord and

AN INNOCENT IMPOSTER 87

Lady Allistair's ball tonight," he said, addressing Lady Mayfield.

"Yes, we do," said her ladyship.

"Oh, excellent!" Mr. Morriville turned to Susan. "Then I beg you to save me a dance, Miss Leighton."

"If you wish, I shall be happy to," said Susan politely.

"Oh, most definitely," said Mr. Morriville. "Perhaps you will save me a Scotch Reel?" he asked and winked at her.

Susan blinked and nodded, and wondered what shenanigans Miss Leighton was up to with Mr. Morriville.

He grinned broadly and told her he would be counting the hours.

"Let us hope he can count that high," said Lady Mayfield after the young man had left. "I hope you don't plan to encourage him, Arabella. The earl would not like it."

To insult poor Mr. Morriville's intelligence seemed uncalled for, and in spite of the fact that she was sure he was up to something Susan felt a sudden illogical need to defend him. "He seems a nice enough man," she ventured.

"And so he would be if you weren't already promised to another," pointed out her ladyship.

Susan bit her lip and wondered if she should say yet again that she wasn't Arabella Leighton.

Her ladyship mistook Susan's silence for a

different sort of contemplation. "Do you begin to see how wrong some of your actions have been, child?" she prompted gently.

All manner of responses swirled in Susan's mind. She longed to cry out that she was not who Lord Mayfield thought she was, that it was wrong to keep judging her by someone else's behavior, that she would prove to them all she was, indeed, Susan Layne, maligned governess. She bit back all responses. What was the use? No one would believe her. She would have to trust time to stand her friend. She sighed. "Your ladyship will excuse me?"

Lady Mayfield's eyebrows rose at this lack of contrition, but she inclined her head and Susan left the room with as much dignity as she could muster, hoping her mama would arrive in London soon to vindicate her.

"I suppose your dances are all promised?" said the earl as they rode to the ball that night.

"I don't believe so," said Susan, and found herself perversely hoping her tormentor would ask her for a dance.

"Well, see to it you don't dance more than once with that wastrel Morriville. If I had been home this afternoon I'd have sent him away with a flea in his ear."

"He did not seem like a wastrel," said Susan.

"He is a wastrel and a fortune hunter," said Mayfield. "I have seen enough of the cub to know he has no loyalties save to himself. He enjoys the hunt, but once the fox is caught he cares naught what becomes of it."

"He is a true Englishman, then," said Susan, who abhorred fox hunting.

The earl frowned. "Do not pretend to be stupid Arabella. You know very well to what I was alluding. For your father's sake I shan't let you be taken in by some sapskull cub who fancies your fortune."

"Perhaps he fancies more than fortune," said Susan, irritated by the earl's judgmental attitude.

"We shan't discuss it further," said the earl.

Really, this man was the most high handed, arrogant . . . "And why not!" demanded Susan.

"Because . . . we just shan't."

"That is no answer."

"It is all the answer I am prepared to give," said the earl ignoring the look his mother gave him. He looked out the carriage window. "Ah, I see we are here," he said pleasantly, as if they had been discussing the weather. "And only ten carriages before us. It is a good thing we left so early. I detest waiting in long lines."

Susan sat and fumed silently. What an odious man the Earl of Mayfield was! She had half a mind to run away, herself. Well, she couldn't run away tonight, but she could, most certainly, dance the Scotch Reel with Mr. Morriville. And a waltz as well!

Susan and her jailers went through the receiving line and made their way to the ballroom. The many hot house flowers which decorated the room made it smell like some exotic paradise and Susan felt her senses reeling as the heady smell mixed with the visual assault of potted palms, flowers and candles, along with the wink and sparkle of jewels and the lush colors of fine gowns. This was how the Upper Ten Thousand lived, amidst extravagance and grandeur. And from this Miss Leighton had run away. How the earl must have mistreated her to force her to such extreme measures!

"Come, Arabella. I will dance the first dance with you," said the earl, holding out his arm.

This was what Miss Leighton had run from, thought Susan, a man who behaved as if his house were France and he Napoleon. "I don't wish to dance just yet," she said, pulling back. "Perhaps you would fetch me some punch."

The earl bowed. "As you wish."

She sat in a chair and unfurled her fan. Already the room seemed warm. The musicians had tuned up and the dancers had taken their places. They began to dance the Quadrille, and Susan watched, enchanted by the spectacle. Across the sea of gowns and faces she caught sight of Miss Thibble and smiled. Blue became her.

"What so entrances you?"

She turned to see the earl had returned with her punch. "Miss Thibble," she said, taking the cup from his hand. "She looks quite nice tonight."

The earl followed her gaze. "By jove, she does," he agreed, surprise in his voice.

Susan smiled, and flirted with the temptation to brag about how she'd guided Miss Thibble in her choice of color. The earl's next words stole the smile from her face.

"You could learn from her, Arabella. She is a sweet girl, neither headstrong nor argumentative."

"Oooh, you wicked man," growled Susan. "If I weren't a lady I should throw this punch in your face."

"Oh, are you a lady now? That is progress, indeed," taunted the earl.

Her tight grip on the cup turned Susan's fingers white. "You truly are a monster," she said.

"One of your making," retorted the earl. "Before your father left to me the dubious honor of acting as your guardian, I was accounted by most to be a very pleasant and reasonable fellow."

"I sincerely doubt that," said Susan hotly. "Obviously, Miss Leighton has managed to test your character, and it would appear to me, your lordship, that you have failed miserably."

The Quadrille had ended and people were drifting off the dance floor. New partners were already taking the floor for the next dance. Mayfield stood and held out his hand to Susan. "We will dance now."

"I shan't," she said.

He reached down, took her hand and tugged her to her feet.

"Let go of me or I shall kick you," she said between gritted teeth.

"And make a scene?" he taunted. "It won't be the first time, will it? How does it feel to be the one who is embarrassed Arabella? That is a new sensation for you, is it not? It is usually you who is embarrassing others." He led her out to the dance floor and forced her to stand there, waiting for the orchestra to begin playing.

"Let me go," she commanded.

"Kick me," he dared her.

"I shall," she threatened.

He shrugged. "I am waiting."

The music began. It was a waltz, and before Susan could decide what to do he had circled his arm around her waist and drawn her out onto the floor. His physical closeness sent tiny tingles in all directions throughout her body, and angry as she felt with him some part of her seemed to be crying out for him to draw her closer yet.

"Does this remind you of another time you waltzed?"

The earl's tone was anything but sentimental and Susan wondered what on earth Miss Leighton had done on the dance floor. "Was it with you?" she guessed.

"Ha! You are witty tonight. The girl who waltzed before receiving permission to do so, the girl who nearly ended her season before it was begun, the girl who put me in the position of penitent to Lady Jersey, that same girl has the nerve to ask if it was I who waltzed with her."

Susan felt as if all eyes were upon them. "Please, your lordship, lower your voice. People are beginning to stare."

The earl looked up, as if suddenly remembering where they were. He smiled down at her, a very insincere smile. "You are upsetting me. I never get upset. We will speak no more now."

True to his word, he waltzed her around the room without another word said, holding her with as much warmth as one might hold a broom.

By the time the dance was over Susan felt exhausted and miserable and ready to cry, and the grinning face of Mr. Morriville was like an oasis in the desert. "Mr. Morriville," she cried happily.

"I have come to claim my dance," he said. "Good evening, Lord Mayfield."

"Good evening, Morriville," said the earl

coldly. He bowed to Arabella and told her to be careful not to become overheated.

"Never fear," said Mr. Morriville, smiling at Susan. "I shall take good care of her."

As Mr. Morriville led Susan away from the earl she felt the energy and enthusiasm he had stolen returning. Here she was at a ball, in a fine gown. She would enjoy herself and worry no more tonight about what the Earl of Mayfield might think of her.

The lively steps of the Scotch Reel left her nearly breathless, and before the musicians had finished their last chord Mr. Morriville was leading her from the floor, winking and saying, "You look terribly overheated Miss Leighton. Shall we step out onto the balcony where the air is cool?"

Susan was, indeed, hot, and the thought of cooling off sounded like an excellent idea. But as soon as she was out on the balcony she discovered Mr. Morriville had not come out to cool off. In fact, his ardour was burning hot. As soon as the door was shut behind them he turned her around and gave her a great, smacking kiss on the lips.

"Mr. Morriville!" she exclaimed, outraged.

Mr. Morriville was not the least bit chastised. He chuckled and took a nibble of Susan's neck.

"Mr. Morriville, you must stop," she remonstrated, trying to squirm away.

"Come now, my dear," he cajoled, "did

AN INNOCENT IMPOSTER

we not agree that Scotch Reel would be our secret word?"

"Oh, my," said Susan faintly.

Mr. Morriville took advantage of her distraction and dove for her neck again.

"Mr. Morriville!" she grunted, struggling to wriggle out of his grasp.

Her captor refused to loosen his hold. "Why are you being such a spoil sport?" he complained.

"Yes," echoed a voice from behind them, "do tell us."

Susan and her amorous companion turned to see the Earl of Mayfield standing in the doorway.

Six

"Lord Mayfield, thank heaven," breathed Susan.

The earl ignored her. "Of course, you realize I could force you to marry this young woman," he said to Morriville.

"No!" gasped Susan.

Mr. Morriville pulled himself up to his full five foot, six inches in an attempt to stand as tall as the stern figure before him. "I am prepared to do the honorable thing," he said.

"I am sure you are as there is a considerable fortune involved," said the earl, "but as Miss Leighton is already promised to Lord Redburrough, you shall have to settle for making your amends on the field of honor."

The younger man's face turned white but he made no protest.

"I am sure Lord Redburrough need never hear of this," put in Susan.

"Arabella, you will please stay out of this," instructed the earl.

"I am not afraid to meet Lord Redburrough," managed the young man.

"Are you not? Then more the fool you,"

AN INNOCENT IMPOSTER

replied the earl. "For he is a crack shot, and I've never known him not to kill his man in a duel."

"But he must not duel with Mr. Morriville, for this is all my fault," said Susan, suddenly inspired.

"Your fault!" chorused both men.

She nodded. "It was my idea to come out onto the balcony. I told Mr. Morriville that if I promised to dance a Scotch Reel with him it meant I wished to, er . . ." Here she stumbled to a halt, feeling too embarrassed to go farther.

The earl's eyebrows met in an angry V. "Go inside and sit with my mother," he commanded.

"What are you going to do?" she asked in a trembling voice.

"Tell this young fool what a lucky escape he has had," growled Mayfield. "Now, leave!"

Arabella left, face flaming. She didn't have to go far, for Lady Mayfield had taken up a seat nearby. "I hope you are happy, young lady," said the countess as Susan sank onto a chair, "for you have caused a great deal of trouble this night, and if you have not compromised yourself it will be a wonder."

"I had no idea what Mr. Morriville meant to do," protested Susan. "I was never so glad to see anyone in my whole life as I was the earl just now."

"Yes, well, I doubt that he will be able to

say he experienced the same sentiments on seeing you. You may have two more dances, then I will develop a headache and we shall leave. I would suggest you pick your next partners more carefully."

"Can we not simply leave now?" begged Susan.

"And give the gossips more to talk of? I think not."

A young man with no chin approached them and timidly asked if Miss Leighton was free for the next dance and her ladyship smiled on him and assured him that Miss Leighton would be delighted to dance with him.

The bogus Miss Leighton smiled weakly and allowed herself to be led off, sure that everything happening to her was punishment for allowing herself to enjoy wearing Miss Leighton's lovely gowns.

The Earl of Mayfield succeeded in scaring Mr. Morriville into silence about his escapade on the balcony, then went in to join his mother. "Well, and have you managed to scotch any scandal?" she asked.

"I believe so," he said. "Really, Mother. If I ever marry I pray I never have girls. They are entirely too much trouble." His gaze followed Arabella about the floor. "I hope we may safely take her home after this dance,

AN INNOCENT IMPOSTER 99

for I have had quite enough for one evening."

"Order the carriage sent 'round," said her ladyship.

As the carriage rolled through the streets of Mayfair the earl kept waiting to hear his charge apologize for her unforgivable behavior. No apology came, and at last he felt the need to pull one from her. "I hope you understand now why I warned you against Morriville in the first place," he said. She remained silent, her eyes on her lap, and he continued, "Do you have any idea what kind of a reputation such brazen behavior will earn you?"

"I did not know he meant to kiss me," she began.

The girl was a liar's delight! "You forget what you said on the balcony," pointed out Mayfield.

"I made that up," said Arabella. "Really, your lordship. You were about to do heaven knew what to Mr. Morriville. I had no idea he had arranged some secret code with Arabella, but it hardly seemed fair to make him suffer for something she—"

"Enough!" commanded the earl. "You really cannot have it both ways, Arabella. You cannot, one moment be you confessing that you arranged an assignation, then the next moment be someone else pretending you were yourself." He stopped a moment, lost in the verbal tangle, then glared at her as if that, too, were her fault.

She jutted out her chin. "I had to do something to save that poor man."

Mayfield could hardly believe his ears. "That poor man only wished to compromise you and get your fortune. He cares not a whit for you. And once he had you he'd be off deflowering some other poor virgin."

"Gerard!" gasped his mama.

"Now look what you have caused me to say," snapped Mayfield. Really, the girl was turning him positively demented. "This is exactly the sort of discussion I tried to avoid on the way to the ball." Arabella slipped a hand up to dab the corner of her eye. Why the devil must she cry as if he had done her some mortal harm? He supposed if he didn't soothe the chit he would have to face his mother's remonstrances later. Mayfield heaved a great sigh. "Arabella. I know you think me a monster, but in truth I am only trying to do what is best for you, to act on your behalf as your own father would if he were alive. Why can you not see that?"

She raised her eyes to his. Lord, but they were the bluest eyes he'd ever seen, and the saddest. "I believe you are," she said. "And I do thank you for coming to my rescue tonight."

Suddenly, Mayfield felt an odd elation,

AN INNOCENT IMPOSTER 101

and a fierce desire to prove to her he wasn't the monster he knew she still thought him.

No, wait! What was he thinking? It mattered not what this vixen thought of him. It only mattered that he get her married off and out of his hair as soon as possible. She was a good example of why ladies should not be educated. Look what they did with the little intelligence they possessed—made assignations with lecherous young fortune hunters, ran away, refused proper suitors!

He realized that Arabella was now watching him warily, as if she'd been able to read his angry thoughts. Well, good. She should understand that the Earl of Mayfield was not a man to anger. And he had other things to do besides follow after Arabella Leighton, always being on hand to save her when her little adventures turned dangerous. "In the future you will be more careful to behave with propriety," he said icily, "for I may not be inclined to rescue you next time."

She turned her face to the carriage window, rewarding him with a view of a trembling lower lip.

I shan't let her melt me with tears, he determined, and turned his head the opposite direction.

As soon as he had safely delivered her and his mother back home, he left them and headed for Brooks' for a night of gambling, sure that cards, fine wine, and sensible male companionship would drive all thoughts of

Arabella from his mind and restore his equilibrium.

Unfortunately, although he won five hundred pounds and returned home pleasantly foxed, thoughts of the pesky Arabella clung to his brain like cobwebs, and the next day he was unable to resist the urge to seek her out.

He found her in the library, reading. "Trying yet again to turn over a new leaf?" he asked.

"Why do you say that?" she replied in that serious manner she had adopted ever since he hauled her back from The Swan.

"Because," said Mayfield, "you would normally be incapable of sitting quietly all day and reading."

"Oh? What would I normally do?"

How the devil should he know? He didn't follow her about. Whatever she did, it was bound to be frivolous. Mayfield shrugged. "Go shopping, pay morning calls, sit before your looking glass and primp."

"My mother always discouraged primping. She said I had no need of it." Here the chit managed a modest blush. "And besides," she added, "Mama always said, 'Pretty is as pretty does.'"

This was not an Arabella sort of thing to say, but the earl could think of no immediate response to it, other than to remind her yet again that her mother was dead. And as she was pretending to be that governess again

AN INNOCENT IMPOSTER

that would do no good, so he settled for a disgusted, "Humph." She was regarding him as if waiting for him to say something more, so he did. "Well, you cannot sit about the house all day. What will you do?"

"What should I do?"

Was the chit now expecting him to entertain her? "How the devil should I know?" he replied. "Ask my mother to take you shopping."

"I have an entire wardrobe full of clothes," she protested.

"Pray, why should that stop you from wanting more?" retorted the earl cynically.

"It seems silly to go out and order more when I have not yet even worn all the things I already have," she said.

She had run mad. That was the only explanation the earl could find for such an outlandishly uncharacteristic statement. He sat down and stared at her.

"You needn't look at me as if I were some odd creature at the zoological gardens," she said, her face growing red.

"You are, indeed, a very odd creature, I assure you," said Mayfield. "And such a statement sounds especially odd coming from the woman who, only five days ago, refused to return Redburrough's ring. Which reminds me, I wish you to give it over to me for safe keeping. Unless, of course, you have changed your mind and intend to marry him."

"Ring?" she prevaricated.

"Yes, ring," said the earl, his temper straining at the bit. "The ruby ring you insisted on keeping after informing me you wouldn't have Redburrough."

She bit her lip and stared at him.

Mayfield felt slightly sick. "Arabella? What have you done with it?"

She made no reply, only bit her lip and looked helplessly at him.

"We have been down this road before, and I am tired of it," he said sternly.

She shook her head. "I wish I could give you this ring you want, but I cannot."

Mayfield felt the blood draining from his face. "What do you mean you cannot? What fresh prank is this?"

"It is no prank. I have no idea what you are talking of," she said. "And I've seen no ruby ring in Arabella's jewel box."

"You have pawned it, haven't you?" Mayfield guessed, feeling increasingly unwell. "You got that smarmy creature I caught you with last night to pawn the thing. My God, Arabella, have you any idea of what you've done?"

"I am not Arabella," she said in a strained voice.

Back to the same weak story. Would she never stop? Mayfield felt his blood beginning to bubble. "Arabella," he said, his voice threatening.

AN INNOCENT IMPOSTER 105

She remained silent, still looking at him helplessly.

With murder in his heart, Mayfield rose and came to tower over her. She shrank back against the chair and it gave him great satisfaction to see fear in her face. "I shall find it," he said between gritted teeth, and you had best pray that no one has bought it, for if I cannot find the thing I shan't whitewash the truth to protect you from Redburrough's wrath when he learns what you have done!"

Having whipped himself into a fine fury, the earl stormed out of the room, calling for his cape and gloves and his curricle. Twenty minutes later, as he drove toward Jew King's in Cranbourn Alley to seek the pawned ring, two visions accompanied him. One was of himself throttling the pesky Arabella. The other, God help him, was of her in his arms. Truly, he must be going mad.

Susan remained for some time, rooted to her chair in the library, her mind running helter skelter in all directions. Where would this all end? What would the earl do when he returned from his futile search for the ruby ring? Would he beat her? He had certainly come close enough this last confrontation. Where was that ring? Had Arabella, perhaps, hidden it in her room, thinking to get it later when things had calmed down?

Susan went to Arabella's room and rang for Brown.

"Do you wish to change, miss?" asked Brown with the eagerness of a novice.

"Brown, I am wondering if you have seen a ring lying about," said Susan.

"A ring, miss? Oh, the. . . ." Brown stopped before going further.

So, thought Susan, the servants had been talking. She considered informing Brown that she wasn't really Arabella, that she, herself, would never keep a gentleman's ring if she didn't mean to have him.

But if she told her maid that she wasn't Arabella, she would have to explain who she really was; Susan Layne, a mere governess, parading about in an heiress's gowns. And while it had been necessary to tell this to Lord Mayfield and his mother, pride assured her it would be impossible to explain her innocence to a fellow hireling. It was true that a governess stood a cut above the rest of the serving class, but she wasn't a lady either. She was a creature neither fish nor fowl, and that was what she was expected to stay, no matter what the popular novelists might write. And such a creature who dared to masquerade as a fine lady could surely expect no moral support from a servant.

Susan tried to sound nonchalant. "I have misplaced a valuable ruby ring. I don't remember seeing it when I was looking through

AN INNOCENT IMPOSTER

my jewel box for something to wear to the ball."

"Perhaps you overlooked it, miss," suggested Brown diplomatically, going to the jewel box.

"Perhaps," said Susan. "If it is not there, look among my gloves."

While Brown searched the obvious places, Susan poked around the room, looking for clever hidey holes. She even went so far as to peek under the mattress of her bed, but to no avail.

After half an hour of searching, Susan plopped onto the bed and sighed. Arabella had taken the ring with her. There could be no doubt of that now.

Brown looked about the room and scratched her head. "Did you look in your portmanteau?" she suggested, then blushed.

Susan blushed, too, knowing the whole household must know that Arabella had run away. "Never mind, Brown," she said. "It was worth a try. I am sure the ring will turn up. You may return at six and help me dress for dinner."

"Yes, miss." Brown bobbed a curtsy and left.

Susan looked around the room one last time, hoping for inspiration, wishing the ring would magically appear. And if it did, then what? The earl would be even more convinced that she was Arabella. Perhaps it was for the best that the thing was as missing as the real Arabella Leighton, she concluded. For at least the fact that she didn't possess it leant credence to her story. And when the earl returned from his futile search of London's pawn shops he'd have to listen to her. She decided to return to the library to wait for him.

When he finally returned he didn't look like a happy man.

"You did not find the ring?" asked Susan.

"No," he replied coldly. "I did not."

"That does not surprise me," she said, her voice equally chilled. "It is nowhere in Arabella's room. I am sure she has it with her."

The earl fell into a chair, threw a booted foot onto the footstool and sighed heavily. "Ah, yes, the girl at The Swan."

"Yes, the girl at The Swan," repeated Susan, trying to sound calm.

"And we have simply to wait for her to reply to your letter, or, better yet, return home, and the mystery of the missing ring will be solved."

Susan nodded.

He studied her, like a man assessing an opponent. "I have a better idea," he said at last.

"And what is that?"

"We shan't sit about waiting for the mystery of your identity to unravel itself. I shall take you to see your mama."

"You will?" This was, indeed, a wonderful idea. Then, at last, the earl would know that

AN INNOCENT IMPOSTER 109

Susan was exactly who she said she was . . . and she'd never see him again. Suddenly, the idea lost some of its charm. And besides, what if her mother were already en route to London?

"Well?" prompted Mayfield.

"My mother might already be on her way here. What if we should miss her?"

"I think we can chance it," said the earl, his voice taunting. "If she should miraculously appear, she may remain in the house as my guest until we return."

"Of course," murmured Susan.

"We shall leave first thing tomorrow morning," he said. "Meantime, tonight we have a ball to attend, and I expect you to be on your best behavior."

Susan searched for some clever rejoinder, but none came to mind, so she settled for letting her face show just how insulting his words were, then left the room.

The ball they attended that night was given by no less a personage than Countess Lieven, and as Susan entered Ashburnham House she felt her quaking legs would never support her long enough to move her through the receiving line. "I feel ill," she confessed to the earl as they inched along.

"Save your vapors for tomorrow when you will need them," he replied heartlessly.

The countess was renowned for her entertainments, which were meant to please the most jaded revelers, and what Susan saw when she entered the ballroom took her breath away. Colored lamps glittered like hidden jewels among the flowers, and the table where a running supper had been laid out was laden with every imaginable food, from imported fruits to ices from Gunthers. In the center of the table was a gigantic spun sugar castle.

Susan didn't have long to stand and admire the scene before her, for the crowd coming into the room behind them moved them on. The musicians were still tuning up and people milled about in clumps, visiting and looking about to see who had been invited.

Beyond a clump of dowagers, Susan thought she caught sight of a familiar scrawny figure and prayed she was wrong. The group of ladies shifted, giving her an open view of the guests behind them and her heart sank as she saw clearly the profile of the honorable Andrew Caine. She turned her back quickly, hoping he wouldn't notice her. In a crowd this size, surely she could manage to avoid Mr. Caine for an evening.

A young man came to claim her for the first dance. "You look even more lovely than usual tonight, Miss Leighton," he said.

"Thank you," she replied absently, and craned her neck to see where Mr. Caine had disappeared.

AN INNOCENT IMPOSTER

The young man tried again. "Are you enjoying the season?"

"What?" said Susan. "Oh, yes. Very much."

The music began, and she still saw no sign of Mr. Caine. She bowed to her partner, then began the steps of the dance, scanning the room one last time. Just as she caught sight of her nemesis at the supper table, filling a plate, the movement of the dance parted the people between them like a curtain, and Susan found herself suddenly exposed to Mr. Caine's idle scrutiny. His eyes widened, then he grinned, and Susan felt her heart fall heavily into her stomach. From the look on his face, it was clear Mr. Caine meant to make a nuisance of himself.

The dance continued and the dancers pulled back together like the red sea, sweeping away the vision of Mr. Caine setting down his plate. Susan's partner smiled at her and she returned it weakly. It was not going to be a pleasant evening.

The dance ended and Susan's partner returned her to Lady Mayfield, who was deep in conversation with a distinguished looking older gentleman. Her ladyship gave Susan a distracted smile, and when Susan's skinny, pimply faced nemesis appeared to claim her hand, the countess waved her carelessly off.

"Well, Miss Layne," said Mr. Caine, strolling Susan along the edge of the dance floor, "I see you progress admirably. From governess in my house to guest of Countess Leiven. I should still like to know how you managed it."

Susan caught sight of Miss Thibble only a few feet away looking at them with interest. "We cannot talk here, she said.

"I know where we cannot be overheard," said Mr. Caine, pulling her along.

Outside, the background of the garden was hung with a transparent landscape of moonlight and water, but all Countess Leiven's artistry was lost on Susan, who, finding herself alone with yet another young man was feeling extremely nervous. If the earl should find her thus again. . . . "This will never do," she said firmly.

"Very well. We will go back inside the ballroom and I shall ask you very loudly what you are doing pretending to be some other woman and living with the Earl of Mayfield," said her companion in a loud voice.

Susan turned and grabbed him by the arm. "Are you mad? Do you want the whole world to hear you?"

He grinned. "Now, that is more like it," he said, leading her into the shadows.

"Mr. Caine," she protested. "I say again, this will never do."

He stopped and put his hands on her waist. "This will do much better," he said, and leered at her.

"I thought you wished to hear my story,"

scolded Susan, trying to pry off his fingers. "This is no way to behave, Mr. Caine."

"This is a perfect way to behave," he replied, and bent to kiss her.

She turned her face away. "You must stop this at once!"

"One little kiss," he begged, and, looking like a fish opening its mouth for the bait, he closed his eyes and tried again. Before he could make contact, she was wrenched from his arms. His eyes popped open to find the Earl of Mayfield glowering at him.

"Might one ask what you think you are doing?" demanded Lord Mayfield.

"Er, that is . . . the lady felt the need of some fresh air."

"My ward seems to need a good deal of fresh air," observed his lordship, looking accusingly at Susan. "But she appears quite recovered now. You may leave her to my care."

"I say," began the youth.

The earl grinned, baring his teeth. "Before I am forced to separate your head from your neck."

Caine made a hasty bow and hurried off.

The earl returned his attention to Susan. "How is it I find you alone with yet another man?"

"It was not my idea, I assure you," she said.

"Oh?"

"It was Mr. Caine's. I am afraid he still thinks me a governess in his house."

"Ah, yes. Miss Layne, the governess."

"Yes, Miss Layne the governess," sighed Susan.

"You are a most convincing actress," said the earl grudgingly.

"Your lordship." Susan laid a pleading hand on his arm.

He looked at it in a detached manner, rather like someone observing a ladybug on his sleeve. Then he took it in his and raised it for a closer examination. "The first two times I saw you, you were biting your thumbnail," he said. "When did you stop biting your thumbnail, Arabella?"

"I have never bitten my fingernails," Susan replied.

The earl raised his gaze from her hand to her mouth. "Your voice. You are still speaking with it lowered. I rather like it," he added absently.

Susan looked at him, mesmerized. "Do you?" she whispered.

"I . . . do." Slowly, as if drawn by some magnetic force, the earl's lips lowered toward hers.

Susan watched as the handsome face drew ever closer, willing him to kiss her, even though it was wrong, even though he was cruel and insensitive and thought her another woman. He could be a monster, yes, but he could also be like . . . this. She tipped her face and closed her eyes.

His mouth hovered within a breath of

Seven

Bright sunlight teased open Miss Arabella Leighton's eyelids, and for the first time she opened them and was acutely aware of many things. She was lying on her back in a strange bed. Her entire body ached horribly, especially her poor head and her left arm, which was bandaged against her body. What had happened?

She remembered drifting in and out of sleep, taking medicine and feeling the sensation of warm, wet flannel that smelt of poppies on her throbbing arm. She remembered a burble of voices, and a large apparition of a woman spooning soup down her throat. Oh, yes. And then there was the handsome face, framed by light brown curls. Was he some relation to her, a husband, perhaps?

She shifted her weight and was rewarded by protests from nearly every part of her body. Why was she in such pain? Where was she? And who was she?

The only thing she was certain of was the fact that she was heartily sick of lying in bed.

AN INNOCENT IMPOSTER 117

In spite of her misery she wanted to be up and exploring. But how could she manage to get out of this homely nightgown alone with her arm all trussed up?

Slowly, she sat up, then waited for her head to stop spinning in protest before rising to cross the bare wood floor and peep out the door. She looked down a long hallway with many other doors. Was she in some sort of inn?

As if in answer to her question, she saw a round faced girl wearing an apron and mob cap over chestnut curls coming down the hall, a bundle of sheets draped over her arms.

"Excuse me," called Arabella.

The girl stopped and regarded her with delight. "Oh, you are up! Mrs. Dickens will be glad to hear it."

"I should like to get dressed," said Arabella. "But I cannot manage alone."

"I will come help you," offered the girl. "Let me just make up this bed and I'll be there in a trice."

Arabella went back to sit on her bed and take stock of her surroundings.

The girl she'd seen a few minutes before knocked on the door then entered the room. "How do you feel?" she asked.

"Everything aches something fierce," said Arabella. "What happened to me?"

"You was in a carriage accident. Don't you remember?"

Arabella shook her head.

"Mrs. Dickens says it's a wonder you wasn't killed, or at least got your arm broke. She had a nephew once, fell from a coach and broke both legs. How is your head? Mrs. Dickens said you got a good bump on it."

Arabella put her fingers to the unnatural protrusion. Just the slight touch made her wince. "It's an awfully big lump," she said.

The girl nodded. "You was in a bad state."

"Where am I?" asked Arabella.

"You are at The Swan, in Reigate. I'm a maid here. My name is Peg Miller."

The girl looked at her expectantly and Arabella opened her mouth to introduce herself, but no name came to mind. "Who am I?" she asked.

"Oh, dear," said Peg. "You still don't know?"

Arabella shook her head, wondering what horrible thing the girl was going to tell her about herself.

Instead, the girl shook her head. "Such a pity you don't know who you are. Well, I suppose it will all come back to you sooner or later."

"You mean . . . you don't know who I am?"

"Lud, no," replied Peg. "We just been calling you poor miss."

Poor miss. What a pitiful thing to be known as, thought the amnesiac. She screwed her eyes shut, hoping the effort would make some name pop into her mind. Nothing came. When she opened them, Peg had produced an ugly gown made of cheap material.

"We will have to unwrap the bandages to get you into your gown," she said, laying the garment on a chair.

Arabella looked at it in distaste. "That is mine?"

The girl nodded.

Arabella sighed and allowed Peg to help her. By the time they had finished, both her arm and head were throbbing, and she had to let her exhausted body lay back down on the bed.

"You'll start to feel better soon," predicted the girl. "I'll come back later and put the lotion what the doctor had Mrs. Dickens make up on that arm. A tablespoon of sol-ammoniac to a quart of vinegar." Arabella wrinkled her nose in distaste and Peg nodded. "Smells right awful, but doctor said it would do the trick." She smiled encouragingly at her patient. "Meanwhile, you just have a good lie-down and I'll go fetch Mrs. Dickens."

Arabella stayed on her bed for some time, too weak to move, too restless of mind to appreciate her prone position. At last she heard the sound of approaching footsteps, and judging from the heavy thumping they made, the feet came with a very large body.

The door opened and the doorway was

filled with a giant of a woman. She had probably been pretty once, but the original shape of her face was now lost somewhere in three chins, and puffy, red cheeks reduced her eyes to the size of currants. Once golden hair was now overrun with gray. The woman had breasts like buckets and hips the size of a horse's.

She gave a great smile and her little currant eyes nearly disappeared. "Well, well, our poor miss is finally awake. And how do you feel?"

"Are you Mrs. Dickens?" Arabella managed.

"None other," said the woman. "How do you feel, dearie?"

"My head hurts, and my whole body aches."

"You are fortunate to be alive to feel anything," said the woman. She clucked her tongue. "Such a nasty accident. And don't think the young scamp who caused it all hasn't been right miserable. Been mooning about ever since it happened, waiting for you to wake up."

The handsome face! "Is he still here, then?" asked Arabella.

Mrs. Dickens nodded and her many chins jiggled. "Been asking about you every day, he has. If you think you're up to it, I will tell him as you will come downstairs for tea later and he can talk to you then."

Something to do besides lie on this small,

AN INNOCENT IMPOSTER 121

lumpy bed and look at the walls! "I should like that," said Arabella.

"Fine then, dearie. You just rest now, and I'll have Peg bring you up an egg and some tea so you can get your strength back."

"Mrs. Dickens," called Arabella.

The woman turned at the door. "Yes?"

"Who am I?"

"You don't know?"

"No."

Mrs. Dickens shook her head at the mystery of life. "Well, lovie, neither do any of us."

"Has no one come looking for me?" asked Arabella in a small voice.

Mrs. Dickens shook her head regretfully. "But never you fear, dearie. I am sure who you are will come back to you once that goose egg on your head shrinks."

Arabella nibbled her thumbnail and tried to remember who she was. Judging from her gown, she supposed she wasn't a fine lady. She considered the cheap, brown material. But surely she had better taste than this!

Her gaze fell on the reticule sitting on the chair by her bed. Was that hers? It must be. And, how very odd. The reticule was much finer than her gown. She supposed she had saved whatever meager funds she possessed to purchase it. She pulled it from the chair and opened it. Inside was a fine, lacy handkerchief, a piece of paper with coach departure times written on it and . . . what was this?

Arabella fished out a gold ring set with red gems. Rubies? What would she be doing with such an expensive ring? Her heart began to thud in panic. Had she stolen it? No, that was impossible. She was sure she wasn't a thief. She couldn't be, for she didn't feel at all like a thief. She put the ring on her finger and examined it. It looked very fine there. It must have been a gift, she decided.

Just then, Peg made her appearance with breakfast—eggs and a thick slab of ham, along with muffins and tea. Arabella smiled. "You may put the tray on this little table," she said.

"Very good, miss," said Peg.

Those words sounded familiar. Some thought tickled the back of Arabella's brain, but refused to come forward. Really, it was most disconcerting not knowing whom one was!

That afternoon Sir Richard Gaine sat at a wooden table out under an apple tree in the inn's courtyard, drinking porter and letting the warm spring sunshine and the buzzing of the bees lull him into a pleasant lethargy, his mind idly turning over the mystery of the young lady. Who could she be? No one had come to The Swan looking for her. She

AN INNOCENT IMPOSTER

was too beautiful to be an orphan. Who were her people?

Sir Richard knew he should have been on his way to London to court Miss Leighton, the heiress he'd heard so much about. If he didn't get there soon, someone would steal a march on him and marry the girl before he'd even gotten an introduction.

But he felt disinclined to leave The Swan. He remembered how lovely the injured girl had looked, with her golden hair spread out on the pillows like the Sleeping Beauty, and reminded himself that it would hardly be gentlemanly to go rushing off and leave the poor thing. After all, it was his fault she got conked on the brainbox.

"Excuse me," said a gentle voice.

Sir Richard turned to see the beauty, herself. She smiled at him, and any final thought of the heiress he so needed to marry to refill the empty family coffers was pushed firmly from his mind. He stumbled to his feet, nearly upsetting his chair in the process and she giggled. He blushed and grinned stupidly at her. She cocked her head, as if waiting for something and, remembering his manners, he introduced himself and took her hand and bowed over it. "Please," he said, rushing to pull out another chair at the table, "won't you join me?"

She sat down and looked about her. "It is very lovely out here," she observed.

"You have the most beautiful hair I have ever seen," marvelled Sir Richard. The girl blushed and lowered her gaze, and he cursed himself and wondered where all his finesse had gone. He was acting like some country dolt. The girl would surely think he hadn't a brain in his head. "That is," he began, and found himself fresh out of clever flatteries. "Er, I don't believe I know your name."

This was obviously the wrong thing to say, for the smile on her face crumpled and her eyes filled with tears. "I don't know it either," she confessed.

Sir Richard's mouth fell open. "You don't know who you are?"

She shook her head, and the tears began to fall in earnest.

Sir Richard fished out his Belcher handkerchief and went to kneel beside her. "Here now," he said, dabbing gently at her cheeks. "You mustn't cry."

"What's to become of me if I don't even know who I am?" she sobbed.

Sir Richard felt the greatest beast in history. It was his fault this poor, sweet creature had no memory of who she was. And how vulnerable that made her! Sir Richard suddenly felt a violent need to protect this poor damsel in distress and make sure no one took advantage of her lack of memory. "There now," he crooned. "Everything will turn out for the best. You shall see. And

AN INNOCENT IMPOSTER

meanwhile you have no need to worry, for I will make sure you are safe."

She looked at him gratefully and sniffed.

"That's better," he said. "And now, let us see a smile."

She obliged and a dimple popped out.

Sir Richard smiled back and took her hand. That was when he saw the ring on her finger. "What is this?" he said thoughtfully.

"I found it in my reticule," she said.

"Here is a possible clue to your identity," said Sir Richard. "It looks old. And valuable. Does it bring back any memories?"

Arabella looked at the ring in distaste. "It makes me unhappy to look at it, but I don't know why."

"Hmm," said Sir Richard. "A mystery, indeed."

Arabella sighed a shaky sigh. "I wish I could remember who I am."

"You will remember eventually, I am sure." Sir Richard patted her hand. "Meanwhile, the sun is out, the birds are singing. It is a lovely spring day, and you need some cider. I shall go in the taproom and fetch some."

Sir Richard scooped his tankard from the table and went to fetch cider for the mysterious woman and more porter for his own mug.

He found the landlord, Mr. Dickens, was there, pouring some liquid fortification for himself. Mr. Dickens was nearly as large as his wife, with a pockmarked face and a bulbous nose made red by many years of sampling the ales he gave to the coachmen who stopped at The Swan.

"Some cider, Mr. Dickens, and another mug of that fine porter."

"Cider, is it?" said Mr. Dickens with a grin. "Is our young lady up and about, then?"

"She is," replied Gaine.

Mr. Dickens filled a pewter mug with cider and gave Sir Richard his porter. He leaned his beefy arms on the old, wood counter and watched Sir Richard sample his drink. "And how is she?" he asked.

"Recovering nicely," replied Sir Richard, scooping up Arabella's cider. "But it looks like she will be your guest for some time yet. I shall pay you for another week."

"That's right good of your lordship," said Mr. Dickens. "Right good."

"Mr. Dickens!" The commanding voice of his wife came drifting into the taproom and Mr. Dickens jumped. "That woman has a voice like a thunderclap," he muttered. "Coming!" he bellered back.

Sir Richard chuckled and took himself off, and Mr. Dickens went to report to his spouse.

By the time he got to the door of the taproom she was there, wondering if he was again standing about jawing with the guests instead of doing his job. "Really, Mr. Dickens, if I were to drop dead from overwork tomorrow, it would be no surprise to me," she informed him. She shoved a stack of letters into his hands. "Here the mail coach has been gone for hours and you have not yet even gotten around to sorting the post. Heaven knows, I do enough of your work. It doesn't seem to be asking too much to expect you to at least see to the mail."

"I was just now on my way," said Mr. Dickens defensively. "l do have to see to the needs of our guests."

"Just don't you go sitting down seeing to your own needs," warned his wife.

"Just don't you forget who wears the breeches in this family," retorted Mr. Dickens after she was well out of earshot.

Shuffling through the letters, he ambled back into the taproom to fetch his mug of stout. Looking at the direction on one, he frowned. "Miss Arabella Leighton," he muttered. "Devil me if I know who that might be. We got no such person here." And he tossed the missive in the rubbish bin.

Eight

Sir Richard invited Arabella to join him for dinner that evening.

"I think that would hardly be proper," she replied modestly, a smile playing at her lips.

"We can easily get 'round that," he assured her. "Tell old Peg who's taken a shine to you that she may sit in a corner and act the chaperone."

"I am sure she will want to return to her own home."

Sir Richard smiled knowingly. "Tell her I will make it worth her while. Every girl likes a chance to earn a little extra blunt."

Still Arabella hesitated, instinctively knowing that to appear too eager would not serve, and wondering how she knew.

Sir Richard took her hand. "Please?" he begged.

"I shall see how I am feeling," she replied.

After keeping him waiting a full half hour that evening, she did make an appearance in the private room, an excited Peg following her through the door.

AN INNOCENT IMPOSTER 129

Sir Richard rushed to greet her. "You came. I am so glad."

"It was most kind of you to invite me," she said, and allowed him to lead her to the table. She looked at her gown in distaste. "I only wish I had something nicer to wear."

Sir Richard regarded the gown critically. "You would look stunning in blue," he observed.

"A blue gown and a Norwich shawl," sighed Arabella. Her eyes suddenly filled with tears. "I do wish I could remember who I am. Surely, no matter who I turn out to be, I must have more than one gown."

"You will remember," said Sir Richard encouragingly. "Meantime, come eat. Mrs. Dickens has provided us with a fine leg of mutton. And look at these tartlets."

Arabella looked at the many delights on the table. The smell of the roast meat mingled with the aroma of beef wafting from a meat pie and fresh mint from Mrs. Dickens' herb garden which had been cooked with tiny new potatoes. Arabella's stomach growled appreciatively.

"Allow me to fill a plate for you," offered Sir Richard.

She sat down and watched him. "I am sure you are used to filling plates for ladies at grand balls and such."

Sir Richard shrugged. "I suppose there have been a great number of grand ladies."

He turned to smile at her over his shoulder. "But none so lovely."

Arabella smiled in return and demurely lowered her gaze to her lap. "I certainly don't look a fine lady," she said.

"But you talk like one."

"Perhaps I should feel more like one if I were better dressed."

Sir Richard set Arabella's plate before her. "The Beau says that clothes make the man. But he would have only to take one look at you to see that isn't true for ladies."

Arabella lowered her gaze. "You are too kind. I hardly feel a lady with my arm all trussed up." Just the mention of her arm made it hurt and she bit her lip.

"Your arm pains you," observed Sir Richard in concern.

"It is nothing," she said nobly.

"I am sure you won't have to endure your difficult circumstances much longer," said Sir Richard.

Arabella sighed. "I hope you may be right, for I am heartily sick of wearing the same thing."

Sir Richard looked suddenly like a man with a secret. "I'd be willing to wager that you won't have to wear that gown for long," he predicted.

Having accomplished what she set out to do, Arabella let the subject drop with a delicate shrug of the shoulders. "Tell me of your home, Sir Richard."

AN INNOCENT IMPOSTER

Now it was the dandy's turn to sigh.

"I have spoken of something that holds unpleasant memories for you," said Arabella, instantly repentant.

"No, no," he assured her. "I have only the most pleasant memories of my home. It is near Northleach, in the Cotswolds, and a more lovely bit of land you'll not find in any other shire. I spent a good many afternoons as a young cub sitting on the banks of the Leach with a fishing pole." He shook his head. "The place is going to rack and ruin, I am afraid."

"Oh, dear," said Arabella, sensing what the problem was.

Sir Richard nodded. "It needs blunt. Something of which we are fresh out."

"And I suppose your family expects you to marry well," said Arabella, trying for a matter-of-fact voice.

He nodded and they both sighed, and Peg, sitting in her corner, looked at them with sympathy.

Sir Richard pulled himself together. "Well. We have grown far too somber. Tomorrow will take care of itself. Is that not how the saying goes? So we shall enjoy today and let tomorrow be hanged." He raised his glass and Arabella did the same. "To tomorrow," he said.

"To tomorrow," she echoed.

Tomorrow came far earlier than Arabella cared for. It seemed she had barely gotten to sleep when Peg was tapping on her door, offering to help her dress. She smiled, remembering her pleasant evening. What new pleasantries would this new day bring?

She found out shortly after breakfast. Mrs. Dickens caught her as she was about to go outside and sit under the apple tree. "Ah, there you are, dearie. Poor lamb. You look bored to death. But never you fear. Old Mrs. Dickens has just the thing to take your mind off your troubles. Follow me."

Arabella followed her down the hall to the back of the inn and into the kitchen. Did Mrs. Dickens have a special treat prepared for her? The sight of the mountain of potatoes sitting on the kitchen table and the huge pot, she soon learned was the treat Mrs. Dickens had prepared.

"This won't take you no time at all," Mrs. Dickens assured her.

"But my arm," protested Arabella.

"You have but to hold the potato with your hand what has the bad arm. The other you can use for peeling."

Arabella sat down in front of the potatoes and stared at them. The prospect of peeling them did not appeal. And how did one peel a potato, anyway? "I am afraid I don't know how to do this," she confessed.

"Everyone knows how to peel potatoes," said Mrs. Dickens scornfully. "It is something you never forget, no matter how hard you are hit on the head. You simply take the knife and peel. Like so." She demonstrated. "Now. You try."

Arabella set her shoulders with determination. With her good hand, she picked up a potato and transferred it to her other hand. Then she picked up the knife and shoved it along the edge of the potato. The knife bounced off, nicking her hand in the process. She let out a yelp and dropped the potato.

Mrs. Dickens shook her head in disgust and bent to pick up the potato.

Arabella sucked on her wounded hand and hoped such proof of her ineptitude would inspire Mrs. Dickens to excuse her from this unpleasant task.

But Mrs. Dickens merely handed her the potato and told her she'd get the way of it.

She waddled to the stack of dirty dishes on other side of the huge kitchen and Arabella stuck out her tongue at the woman's retreating back. She glared at the knife as if the thing had, of its own volition, cut her, then picked it up again and set to work to conquer the potato.

It seemed to Arabella that she sat peeling potatoes for hours. At last, as she picked up her last one Mrs. Dickens announced her intention to go out into the herb garden and cut some chives. She lumbered out the door and Arabella took her remaining unpeeled potato and buried it at the bottom of the pot and made her escape.

She spied Sir Richard in the hallway, whip and hat in hand, obviously ready to go out. He broke into a smile at the sight of her. "Good morning," he called and hurried to take her hand.

"Good morning, Sir Richard. I see you are about to go out."

"I must run some errands," he said, and Arabella was disappointed he didn't ask her to accompany him. Surely he must know she would like some fresh air. "I hope you shan't be averse to company later this afternoon?" he added.

"I am sure I should enjoy it," she said, modestly lowering her eyes.

"Excellent! Until then, your servant." He bowed over her hand and headed down the hall with a purposeful stride.

Arabella stood for a moment, admiring his fine physique. What a handsome man Sir Richard was!

"Oh, there you are, my dear," came a voice behind her. She turned to see Mrs. Dickens thundering down the hall toward her. "You should have come and fetched me when you were finished with the potatoes. I would have found more for you to do."

Arabella remembered the laundry she'd seen simmering in the copper over the huge fireplace and could well imagine what sort of work Mrs. Dickens had in store for her. "I think I have worked enough for one day," she said.

AN INNOCENT IMPOSTER 135

"Tut, tut, girl. We must all do our fair share," said Mrs. Dickens.

"I have definitely done mine today," said Arabella. "And besides, my arm is hurting."

"Well, now. The best thing to take your mind off your hurts is a little hard work, I always say."

"That may be what you always say," replied Arabella firmly, "but I am sure I would say no such thing. I am going to my room now to rest."

Arabella turned and strolled off, leaving Mrs. Dickens to stare after her. "Well," huffed the woman. "Of all the insolent, ungrateful girls!" At that moment her husband happened by. "Did you ever see the like?" demanded Mrs. Dickens.

He shrugged. "Perhaps she's a great lady and not used to work."

His wife gave a scornful snort. "More like she's a lazy maid who is enjoying her holiday at others' expense."

"As long as the young dandy continues to pay her shot, 'tis no skin from my nose," observed Mr. Dickens.

"Did he pay another week?"

Mr. Dickens nodded. "That he did, lovie."

Mrs. Dickens smiled, then sobered and held out her hand. "I'll take the money Mr. Dickens, before it gets gambled away at some cock fight."

"Mrs. Dickens, you wound me," protested her husband.

"I certainly will if you don't hand over the money," said his wife.

Mr. Dickens obeyed, and as his wife moved off muttered that he might just do like the young miss; go off somewhere and forget who he was.

Susan watched out the carriage window and fidgeted with her reticule as Lord Mayfield's footman ran through the pelting rain up the walk past old French roses backed by lilac and pilars of fastigate yew to the cottage door. It had been balm for her spirit driving down the familiar streets of Crawley, and she'd hoped for a glimpse of some of her friends or neighbors. But the rain had kept them indoors. She thought she'd seen the curtain at the house of their nearest neighbor, Mrs. Thomas move as the carriage slowed past. But the chilled spring rain was pouring so hard that even for an earl, no one seemed inclined to come out of their houses.

Now the footman was knocking on the door. Alice, their maid opened it and looked with amazement on the man in the green livery, then past him to the carriage. She stepped back and opened the door wide and the man turned and ran back to open the carriage steps.

"There," said Susan. "That alone should prove my identity, for a stranger would hardly open her door to us."

AN INNOCENT IMPOSTER

The earl gave her a cynical look. "The woman would be a fool not to take advantage of a visit from an earl." He climbed out and handed down Susan and Lady Mayfield and the three ran for the door.

"Alice," said Susan, as soon as they were inside. The girl was too busy staring at the earl to answer. "Where is my mother?" demanded Susan, taking her arm and giving it a shake.

The girl turned to Susan and blinked and managed a curtsey. "I beg your pardon?" she stammered.

"Oh, really," said Susan in disgust. "Will you please show us into the sitting room?"

"Who is it?" called a voice down the hall.

"Mother, it is I," answered Susan.

A puff-chested little butterball of a woman with faded yellow hair trotted into view. At the sight of Susan and the earl and his mother she stopped short.

"Mama!" cried Susan and ran to hug her.

The woman reluctantly accepted Susan's embrace, looking awkwardly at Lady Mayfield, who exchanged looks with her son.

Susan felt the stiffness in her mother's hug and drew back to look at her. "Mama?"

"I am sorry," said the woman, looking to the earl as if for help. "But I am afraid you must have me confused with someone else."

Nine

Susan stared at her mother in disbelief. "Mama, this is no time to jest."

The woman flushed and lowered her gaze. "I am sorry," she murmured.

"No," said Mayfield. "It is I who should apologize for troubling you. Come, Arabella." He gestured with his hand for her to precede him out the door.

Instead, Susan rushed to the maid, who had been trying to make her escape and grabbed her by the arm. "Alice! Tell the earl who I am," she commanded.

The girl shot a look at Mrs. Layne, then replied, "I am sorry, miss."

Susan turned a pleading face to the earl, who now appeared very stern. "She is my mother, I tell you!" she cried. "She is . . ." From far off Susan heard little bells. Fireworks sparkled at the edges of her eyes. Then it was night and she was falling, her limbs like a rag doll's.

From a great distance she heard Alice exclaim, "Oh, she's fainted right away, she has."

AN INNOCENT IMPOSTER

Everyone seemed to be talking at once now. Susan could hear the earl muttering, "Blast the chit," and Lady Mayfield urging, "Pick her up, Gerard." Somewhere in the background was her mama's voice, saying, "Alice, fetch the hartshorn."

She felt herself scooped up and heard the earl apologizing once more to her mother for having troubled her.

"Oh, dear," fretted Mrs. Layne. "If your lordship would care to bring her into the sitting room . . ."

Mayfield cut her off. "We'll not trouble you further, madam."

"But she has fainted," protested Mrs. Layne.

"And she will revive in my carriage. I'll not impose on your generosity further."

I must cry out, thought Susan, but her body was a crypt and she was buried alive. The earl bore her off.

In the carriage, something pungent and nasty was waved under her nose, making the bells tinkle away, leaving her free to open her eyes. She was instantly aware of the earl's face bending over her.

"Better now?" he asked.

She moaned and shut her eyes again. "My own mother has denied me."

"Your own mother?" scoffed the earl. "Why did you pick that particular, unfortunate woman? Did you like the look of her cottage? I'll grant you it is a pretty one, Arabella, but really, you should have planned more carefully."

"And I suppose I *planned* to faint just now."

"It is a useful ruse," said the earl.

Susan drew herself up to a full sitting position in spite of her woozy head. "Really! This is preposterous. Can you think anyone in their right mind would plan such a hoax?"

The earl looked at her thoughtfully. "Perhaps not," he said slowly.

Her eyes widened at the implication behind the words. "You vile man," she breathed.

"I? You drag me clear to Crawley for more of your tricks and you have the nerve to call me names, brat? I shall turn you over my knee." He moved in Susan's direction.

"Gerard!" scolded his mother. "That will be quite enough."

"Really, Mother. She is enough to try the patience of a saint."

All manner of retorts sprang to mind, but Susan realized that saying any of them would only serve to make her look like the wicked Arabella, so she bit them back. She squeezed herself up against her corner of the coach and turned her face to the window. What was she going to do now? she wondered. Disowned by her own mother, what would become of her? Panic primed the pump and

AN INNOCENT IMPOSTER

her tears flowed. Soon she was crying in earnest, unable to stop.

"Arabella. Get a hold of yourself," commanded the earl.

"I cannot," sobbed Susan.

Lady Mayfield moved across to sit next to her and put an arm about her, and Susan accepted the gesture, turning her face into her ladyship's shoulder. "There now," cooed the countess. "It is all right, child."

"Really, Mother," said the earl in disgust. "You should not humor her."

"Let us stop at the George and have something to eat," suggested her ladyship. "I am sure we could all use some tea."

"By all means, let us reward the chit for her behavior. And let us have some tartlets as well."

Her ladyship smiled. "An excellent idea, Gerard."

Susan longed to suggest they stop at The Swan in Reigate, but under the present circumstances she knew how that suggestion would be met. And who could blame the earl, really. Her mother had just succeeded in making Susan appear a madwoman. Possibly, before this tangle was unwound she would be!

Sir Richard returned to The Swan bearing two boxes wrapped in ribbon under his arm. He poked about the inn looking for the beautiful amnesiac but saw no sign of her. At last he went back to the kitchen, where he found Mrs. Dickens, rolling out a pastry crust. "Mrs. Dickens. Have you seen our mystery lady?" he called.

"She is in her room," replied Mrs. Dickens. "Resting," she added with scorn.

"Thank you," said Sir Richard and bounded off, passing Mr. Dickens and wishing him a cheery good day.

"Well, and I wonder where he is off to so chipper and with such boxes under his arm as look to have ladies' finery in 'em," said Mr. Dickens, sauntering up behind his wife to take a pinch of dough.

She slapped away his hand. "As if you cannot guess, Mr. Dickens. Really, I should go upstairs and make sure nothing happens that shouldn't. After all, we run a good, clean inn."

"That we do," agreed her husband, managing to get another bite of dough. His wife frowned at him and he grinned at her and said, "So what keeps you from going up there? I know you are dying to see what is in them boxes."

Mrs. Dickens gave a self righteous snort. "I have things to do, and if naughty girls who refuse to pitch in and help those who have been so kind to them go and get themselves into trouble, then I am sure it is no concern of mine."

"And I am sure you are right," agreed

AN INNOCENT IMPOSTER 143

Mr. Dickens wisely. He reached again for the dough and got his hand roundly slapped for his trouble.

Upstairs, Sir Richard tapped on Arabella's door. "Miss. It is I, Sir Richard."

"Sir Richard?" came the soft voice from the other side of the door. "Oh, gracious. Just one moment."

Sir Richard smiled, imagining the girl, running to the looking glass to check her hair and pinch color into her cheeks. At last the door opened and there she stood, those soft cheeks kissed with rose-petal pink, the blue eyes open in surprise. "May I come in?" he asked.

She seemed undecided.

"I'll only stay a moment," he promised. "I have something for you."

Her eyes went to the parcels under his arm and she smiled and stepped aside for him to enter. "You may come in only for a moment," she said.

Sir Richard laid the boxes on the bed. "The other night when we were dining, you mentioned the sad fact of only possessing one gown."

"Is this for me, then?"

He nodded.

With childlike enthusiasm she tore open the first box and held up a white fringed shawl. He watched her finger the soft fabric. She smiled coyly at him. "It is very lovely."

"Open the other," he said.

She opened the second one and pulled aside the tissue paper to reveal a light blue, muslin gown with puffed sleeves and blue ribbon. She pulled it out and hugged it to her and looked at Sir Richard as if she could not quite believe her good fortune.

"Hold it up to you," he said. She complied and he nodded his approval. "It is as I thought. You look incomparable in blue."

The flush of excitement on her cheeks deepened. "You are too kind," she murmured. She fingered the gown. "I don't know how I can thank you."

Sir Richard came to take her hand. He raised it to his lips and kissed it. "I wish you would allow me to buy you many more gowns."

"I could hardly do that," she said modestly.

"Are you sure? I would like to . . . take care of you," he murmured and put his hands on her waist.

She froze.

She simply needed melting. Sir Richard placed a kiss at the base of her neck.

She turned to face him, wanting him to kiss her no doubt. But when Sir Richard saw her face, he realized that was not at all what she wanted.

"Perhaps you would be so kind as to tell me plainly what you are implying, sir?" she demanded, her chin rising.

Sir Richard felt an unpleasant warmth on

his face. "Well, only that, er, that is . . . I thought you would not be averse to being under my protection."

"Is this a proposal of marriage?"

"Marriage?" he stammered, and dropped his hands from her waist.

She flung the gown onto the bed. "I thought not! How dare you insinuate that I would be the kind of woman to whom a man would make such an indecent proposal!" she cried. Now she was searching angrily about her for something.

Sir Richard had kept enough women in his time to know what that portended and hastily backed toward the door.

She scooped up a hairbrush and hurled it at him. He ducked and it hit the door instead of his head. The girl had remarkably good aim. He decided not to remain behind to give her a second try at taking off his head. This was obviously not the time for apologies. "Beg pardon," he managed, and bolted, shutting the door just in time to hear the thud of an object against it.

Sir Richard went down to the private parlor and plunked himself onto a chair to think. One thing he now knew for certain. The pretty amnesiac was no ladybird.

The morning following the disastrous call on her mother, Susan left her room determined on a new campaign. She would find

Lord Mayfield, sit him down and have a calm talk with him, laying out in a rational manner all the facts in a concise and logical way. If she but spoke rationally to him. . . .

Had she not tried this before? It never worked. Yet what other options had she, other than waiting for the real Arabella to respond to her letter? And what if the real Arabella did not? Could not? What if something terrible had happened to the real Arabella as a result of her accident? Perhaps she was immobilized. For all Susan knew the poor creature could still be unconscious.

Fresh guilt assailed Susan. The real Miss Leighton lay at The Swan on a bed of pain, while she, the imposter danced at balls and attended the opera. The sooner she found a way to put an end to this masquerade, the better! She went in search of the earl.

She found him in the front hallway, about to go out. "Oh," she said, stopping on the staircase. "I see you are leaving."

"What is it you wish Arabella?" he asked in a tired voice.

Susan shook her head. It would hardly put the earl in a receptive mood to upset his plans for the day. "It can wait."

"I'd rather we not," he said. "It would only bedevil me wondering what fresh tricks you are up to now and I should never be able to enjoy myself at Jackson's. Come, let us go into the drawing room."

Once in the drawing room, seated opposite

the earl, Susan found herself unsure of how to begin.

Mayfield did nothing to help her, only sat with one booted leg slung over the other, thrumming his fingers against his thigh impatiently.

She swallowed and said, "I fear that ever since we met we have labored under some grave misconceptions of one another's character."

The earl raised an eyebrow but said nothing.

Susan tried to ignore the nervous hammering of her heart. "I am afraid I allowed my opinion of you to be colored by your ward's description, and saw you for an ogre . . ." He appeared none too pleased with this remark, but still made no comment, and Susan rushed on, "rather than seeing you as a man whose patience had been severely tried by a strong-willed young woman."

He looked surprised. "This is the first sensible thing I have heard you say since I brought you back from The Swan," he said. "I am glad you now see the truth about yourself."

"Not myself," corrected Susan. "Arabella."

The earl set his jaw and looked at his lap. Susan could tell he was preparing to lecture her. Sure enough. "My dear," he said, leaning forward to take her hand in his, "you must get ahold of yourself. See where this game has led you? It has taken hold of your mind. You will only make yourself ill if you persist."

Now he was petting the top of her hand. It had a strangely calming effect, making her body feel like warm honey poured through it.

"It has been a very amusing game, but now it is ended. We will call a truce, give back the ring to Redburrough . . ."

The red haze that descended on Susan obliviated all plans to be calm and logical with Lord Mayfield. "Oooh, that dreadful ring!" she cried snatching away her hand. "If you so much as mention it to me again . . ."

The earl leaned forward. "Yes?" he taunted.

Susan clamped her lips shut.

"You have lost, Arabella. Admit defeat."

"Admit defeat?" she mocked. "Attend the balls, play the part, flirt with every man I see, act the spoilt creature with no conscience . . ."

"Just as you have been doing since I brought you back," jibed Mayfield, and was rewarded with a ringing slap.

Susan stood and looked haughtily down at him. "You are a blind fool," she informed him coldly. "And if harm comes to the real Arabella because of your obstinance, it shan't be on my conscience but on yours." She then sailed from the room, leaving the earl to rub his cheek and stare after her.

His mother entered as Susan was leaving

AN INNOCENT IMPOSTER 149

and received a flustered curtsey and a few polite words before the girl moved on. Her ladyship came and sat down on the sofa, an inquiring eyebrow raised. "What has happened to your face, Gerard?"

"She slapped me," said the earl in disbelief.

"Rather a violent child."

"She has come unhinged," observed Mayfield. "I shall have to let Redburrough off the hook."

"A very wise idea," agreed her ladyship.

Her words sounded slightly tainted with sarcasm and caused her son to look at her questioningly. She merely smiled at him, and he sighed and rubbed his forehead. "There is something not right about all this," he announced.

"Is there?"

He nodded. "The girl has changed since I brought her home."

"How?" prompted her ladyship.

Mayfield shrugged. "That is what bothers me. I am not exactly sure how. I cannot seem to put my finger on it. She is just . . . different."

"I'll warrant she's not been quite what I expected," said Lady Mayfield. "No stamping of feet, no pouting."

"Yes," said Mayfield slowly. "Except for this one violent attack . . ."

"Why did she slap you?" asked her ladyship.

Feeling unaccountably guilty for his words

to Arabella, Mayfield let his eyes slide away from his mother's penetrating gaze and hedged, "A slight misunderstanding."

"I see," said her ladyship in a knowing voice that her son found quite irritating. She was silent a moment, then asked, "How else does the girl seem different?"

The earl scratched his head, trying to remember as much as he could of the old Arabella. "I honestly don't know," he said. "Her behavior is, on the surface, that of Arabella, for I still find her doing things she knows she should not. But what she says when I reprimand her, the way she behaves . . . Ahh, it all goes back to this ridiculous story she has made up! The truth is, she is still the same spoilt, selfish vixen, who does not care to have her will thwarted."

"Is she?" wondered her ladyship. "Tell me again. On how many occasions were you actually with Arabella before she ran away?"

"Enough to know her when I see her. Really, Mother, for what kind of dolt do you take me?"

"Why I don't take you for a dolt at all," said Lady Mayfield. "Only for a typical human being who sees only what he expects to see. Which is . . . to be expected."

The earl was too irritated by his mother's suggestion to appreciate the humor in her clever turn of a phrase.

"Life does not always present us with the ordinary," continued her ladyship calmly.

AN INNOCENT IMPOSTER   151

"Sometimes we must make allowances for the extraordinary."

"There is nothing extraordinary about Arabella," said Mayfield dismissively. "Except, perhaps, her beauty. And it is hard to appreciate that when her behavior is so very vexing."

"Her kindness to Miss Thibble," suggested his mama. "Was that something you would expect from Arabella?"

Mayfield sighed and slumped against the sofa cushions. "No," he said at last. "It does not seem like the Arabella I know to be concerned with improving another woman's looks." A sudden thought flickered at the back of the earl's mind, then vanished like a ghost before he could get hold of it. He strained for a moment, trying to bring it back but it wouldn't come and he sighed wearily and shook his head. "Perhaps it is not the girl who is going mad but I, for I could almost begin to believe her."

Her ladyship patted his arm. "Don't fret, dearest. Your mother has lived a good many years more than you, and experience dictates that things will work out. Somehow, they always do."

The earl gave a cynical snort. "I am sure there are a good many people in Bedlam whose relatives gave them just such comfort right before they went 'round the bend."

* * *

Arabella sat in her room, wrapped in her fine new shawl, fingering the fringe and trying to decide how long she would make Sir Richard Gaine suffer for his crime. A day? Two, perhaps. She would not speak to him, not even acknowledge his existence. He would have to come to her on bended knee before she would forgive him.

She looked at her new muslin gown, draped over a chair. Now, there was a gown much more suited to her taste than the one she had been wearing. Perhaps, with such excellent taste, she was a fine lady?

She certainly knew she was not a scullery maid. She had no aptitude for peeling potatoes. Was she a lady's maid? She hoped not. She would much rather be a fine lady. Sir Richard's boyish face came to mind. She wouldn't at all mind being Sir Richard's fine lady. In spite of what he'd said about his crumbling home, he was obviously rich enough to buy extravagant presents. Sir Richard would make an admirable husband . . . If she didn't already have one!

As Lord Mayfield tooled his curricle down the street he wished he could as easily escape his thoughts as he could his house, for the pesty Arabella refused to be left behind. She followed him from Jackson's to Tattersall's and back home again, and by the time he climbed his front steps he was cursing his

AN INNOCENT IMPOSTER

old friend, Sir Ralph, for ever having had a daughter.

He cursed Sir Ralph yet again when, sifting through the correspondence Childers had left on his desk, he found a letter from the Earl of Redburrough. Back in London in a week. Good God! What was he going to tell Redburrough? And how was he going to get his hands on that curst ring before Redburrough returned. What the devil had Arabella done with it!

The earl rubbed his aching head. And what was he going to do with Arabella? If only she was someone else. He knew what he would like to do with her . . .

The vision of Arabella's earnest face when they first sat down to talk earlier that day came to mind. She had been hesitant to detain him when she saw he was ready to go out. Such consideration was rare in any female, but especially so in Arabella. Or so he'd always thought. Could his mother really be right. Could a woman keep up a pretense and behave in a manner so foreign to her for such a long time? Mayfield chewed his lip. He decided to observe her carefully that evening.

Before leaving for a ball, they dined en famille, making it easy for him to closely scrutinize Arabella's behavior. She was looking pale, he noticed. Perhaps, she had merely worn that cream-colored gown to create the illusion of paleness. She looked more ghost than human. She may as well have been a ghost, for she was contributing little to the conversation, thought Mayfield irritably, watching her toy with her food. "Is the turbot not to your liking?" he asked.

She gave a start. "Oh, no," she managed. "It is quite good." Her eyes drifted away. "I am afraid I am not hungry."

"Perhaps you are going into a decline," suggested Mayfield.

She refused to rise to the bait. "I am simply not hungry, your lordship. Although the turbot is excellent."

"Humph," said the earl.

"It appears Miss Thibble has found a suitor," interjected Lady Mayfield.

"The Earl of Guildford?" guessed Arabella.

Her ladyship nodded.

"I remember making his acquaintance," said Arabella. "He seems an amiable man. I hope he offers for her."

"He is rich as Croesus," put in Mayfield slyly, watching for Arabella's reaction.

"Then Miss Thibble will have no worries if she marries him, " said the girl simply.

Most odd, thought Mayfield. No snide remarks about how undeserving of her good luck Miss Thibble was, no bragging of how Arabella, herself, could have had Guildford if she wanted. From what he'd seen of his ward, such behavior, or lack of it, definitely seemed out of character.

AN INNOCENT IMPOSTER 155

He waited until they were at the ball to bring up the subject of her groom-to-be, waited until they were waltzing. The half of him that was going insane longed to offer her flattery and amusement, to make her laugh. The sane half of him said, "I have had a letter from Redburrough today," and watched for her reaction.

Every last drop of blood seemed to drain from her face. "Pray, what does his lordship write?" she asked in an even voice.

"Why, that he can hardly wait to return to London and see the woman who has made him the happiest man on earth. You have a week, Arabella. What do you say to that?"

She bit her lip and looked away. Then she shrugged fatalistically and said, "I say, let us dance and be merry, for tomorrow we shall die."

"Very well," said Mayfield. "Let us do exactly that, for when Redburrough returns and finds his ring has vanished you will, most likely, wish to die."

She made no comment.

"You are a stubborn child," said Mayfield.

"I am neither of those things, your lordship. I am a woman of scruples." She smiled, and the earl wondered how a smile could look so sad. "I hope I may yet find a way to prove it to you."

"Return Redburrough's ring," said Mayfield softly, "and that will be proof enough."

"I wish I could," she replied, her voice choked.

Mayfield had to fight off the urge to shake her right there on the dance floor until her golden curls came completely undone, until she was begging for mercy, until . . . Oh, God, how he longed to kiss her. Bah! "I have had enough," he said through gritted teeth and ended their waltz. Without another word, he escorted her back to his mother. "I have now done my duty and danced with my ward," he announced. "If you should need my assistance, Mother, I will be in the card room." With that he left the girl and headed off to another part of the house to restore his equilibrium with the logical company of sensible males.

Several of his acquaintance had taken refuge in a salon set aside for those who preferred cards to dancing, and he found himself instantly hailed and invited to participate in a game of Whist. "So you have escaped from guard duty," joked his friend, Sir James Cranston.

Mayfield took a chair. "What I have done that Providence should so chose to punish me I cannot imagine."

The other men chuckled and Sir James, a man with little fortune or looks to put him in any danger from attention by the opposite sex, said, "A sensible man will keep a bit of muslin and have nothing to do with the rest of the petticoat line."

AN INNOCENT IMPOSTER 157

"Allow me to remind you that this particular connection was none of my seeking."

"If your friend had steered clear of parson's mousetrap in the first place you would not now be paying the consequences."

Mayfield merely shook his head. Normally his Cranston's witticisms would be highly amusing. Tonight they were merely aggravating.

"Funny thing," said Sir James, arranging his cards. "I caught sight of a girl last summer who looked remarkably like that ward of yours."

Mayfield's heart stopped. "Where?"

"Let me think. Where was it?"

"Wight's?" prompted Mayfield.

Sir James snapped his fingers. "By damn, that's it! At some house party. M' sister dragged me there. Needed another male, that sort of thing. Anyway, saw this yaller haired beauty walking with the child and asked about her. Turned out she was only the governess."

Only the governess. Miss Layne, the governess. Could it be possible? Mayfield felt suddenly ill. No, he told himself firmly. Accidents of mistaken identity occurred only in silly novels written by females with too much imagination, not in real life. "Play a card, Cranston," he said. "If I wished gossip I would have remained in the ballroom."

Sir James shrugged and complied.

Lord Mayfield sat for half an hour, fiercely

determined to enjoy the game. But enjoyment eluded him, so he gave up and wandered back to the ballroom.

Arabella, or whoever she was, now danced with a young buck who was looking at her as if she were Diana, the goddess of love. She gave him a merely polite smile in return. It was hardly the sort of smile the flirtatious Arabella would offer an admirer.

Mayfield raked a hand through his hair. This was insane. No! He would not even use that word. He had to be dreaming. Tomorrow he would wake up and life would be as it was before Arabella came into his life.

A friend hailed him and he suffered through a conversation about cock fighting, wondering how he was able to endure it when he wanted more than anything to simply indulge himself in one thunderous roar.

The dance ended and the mass of people shifted, couples drifting off the floor. They had been here long enough, Mayfield decided. He excused himself and went in search of Arabella. He would escort her and his mother home, then he would go on to see his little ballet dancer. By now she should be done performing and back at the house he'd rented for her. He hadn't seen her since Arabella turned his world upside down, and he now realized what he needed more than anything was to visit his mistress and spend some time in a world where he was master and life ran along predictable paths.

Arabella made no protest when he informed her that they would be leaving. "As you wish," she said courteously, and that angered him afresh.

"You don't wish to stay longer?" he asked. "Supper will soon be served."

"I shan't starve without it," she replied. "And I have already had an enjoyable evening. More enjoyable than I deserve," she added, as if to herself.

Saint Arabella, thought Mayfield irritably, and pretended not to have heard.

He returned the ladies home, but told the coachman to wait.

"You don't come in, Gerard?" asked his mother.

"No," said the earl. "I have another appointment."

"Very well. Goodnight, my son." Her ladyship gave him her cheek to kiss, which he did, then hurried away.

His little brown-eyed beauty greeted him with delight, bringing him wine, telling him how very handsome he looked. Arabella had never told him he was handsome. Did she, perhaps, think him old?

"I have not seen you in a very long time." Gizelle pouted prettily.

The pout reminded Mayfield of Arabella. The old Arabella. He was not sure this new one was capable of molding her lips in such a fashion.

"My lord?" Gizelle's voice pried his attention away from his thoughts.

"I have neglected you shamefully," he said. "Come sit on my lap."

Gizelle smilingly obliged and began to search his pockets. "And what did you bring your Gizelle to show her how sorry you are for leaving her lonely?"

"Nothing, I'm afraid," said Mayfield, wondering how he could have been so stupid. Again, she produced a pout. "But I promise, my sweet, that I will make it up to you and send you something tomorrow."

"And tonight . . ." She pulled the diamond stick pin from his cravat and stuck it into a sofa pillow, then untied the neckcloth. "You will show me in another way how sorry you are you have neglected me, No?" She kissed him, then frowned. "You are here but you are not," she observed. "What troubles my lord?"

"Gizelle. Do you find me old?"

She smiled, the smile of the courtesan. "I find you just right, my lord."

The earl rewarded her with a kiss and wished her hair was gold.

Back at his house, his mother had persuaded Susan to join her in a late supper. Susan toyed with an oyster and wished there were some way she could induce the countess to share some clues which would unravel the mystery that was Lord Mayfield, that would explain why one moment he seemed to want to kiss her and the next to put her over his knee. "How did your son come to be Arabella's guardian?" she asked at last.

"Sir Ralph and Gerard were officers together. They became good friends. I suppose Sir Ralph felt confident that Gerard would be well able to protect his daughter from fortune hunters. In fact, I am sure Sir Ralph never intended Gerard to become so closely embroiled in his daughter's affairs, but Sir Ralph's sister proved quite unable to control her." The countess took a sip of tea, allowing Susan time to digest this bit of information. "My son actually had little dealings with Arabella personally, but the few he had, it would appear, were not pleasant."

"I see," said Susan slowly. "And why did they argue? Was it because of the ring?"

Lady Mayfield nodded. "It is part of a set; the Redburrough rubies. Arabella took a fancy to the ring—unfortunately, not to the giver."

"Did this poor girl have no redeeming qualities?" asked Susan in amazement.

"I should think everyone has some redeeming qualities," replied her ladyship. "I am not sure my son would agree with me, however."

Susan frowned. "Such a horrible tangle." Almost to herself she added, "I wish your son did not hate me so."

A smile grew on her ladyship's face. "It is only this matter of the ring that makes things difficult."

"All this trouble for a red stone wrapped in a bit of gold," sighed Susan.

Her ladyship leaned back and studied Susan's face until Susan blushed. "Most remarkable," she said at last. "Either you are clever beyond all creatures, child, or you are a victim of the most amazing of circumstances."

Susan looked at her with hope. "You believe me?" she asked eagerly.

"Perhaps," replied her ladyship noncommittally. "I must admit, I begin to think something strange is occurring."

"Will you speak to your son on my behalf, then?"

"I think not," said Lady Mayfield.

Susan looked at her, stunned. "But you have just said . . . Why won't you speak on my behalf?"

"For the simple reason that there is no need," Lady Mayfield replied.

"I am afraid I don't understand."

"It is simple," said her ladyship. "If you are Arabella, you will soon come to realize you cannot pretend to be someone else indefinitely. A young man will offer for you and you will give up the ring and the charade. If, on the other hand, you are Susan Layne, that, too, will be proven in time."

"I *am* Susan Layne," insisted Susan, "and

the woman we saw in Crawley was, indeed, my mother."

"I saw a resemblance," said Lady Mayfield.

"Yet you will say nothing to your son?"

"I know nothing for certain," replied Lady Mayfield. "I have spoken to my son. He believes you to be Arabella."

"And why should he not when my own mother denies me," said Susan bitterly. "What possible reason could she have had for so humiliating her own daughter?"

"If that daughter has been mistaken for an heiress and is about to be married to a title? Come now. What mother would not thank Providence and play along?"

Susan sat stunned. "Do you mean to say you think my mother . . ."

"Why should she not?"

"But that is preposterous!" Susan exclaimed.

Her ladyship shrugged. "This entire situation is preposterous. But I suppose that makes it no less possible."

"And what of the real Arabella?"

"I suspect she has landed on her feet," said Lady Mayfield calmly.

Susan found such lack of concern distressing. "I can assure your ladyship it was not her feet she landed on when she was thrown from the coach."

Lady Mayfield chuckled. "And I can assure you, my dear young woman, that no matter what hard surface the real Arabella encountered when she fell, she is now enjoying a soft life at The Swan. Else we should have heard from her."

"But how can you know?" fretted Susan.

"Because I know the type."

"I cannot like this," said Susan.

"I grow to like it more by the minute," said her ladyship. She looked into the fire and her voice softened. "Oh, I will admit I had my dreams of a fine match for my son. But Gerard has always taken his own path in life. And if I couldn't stop him from donning regimentals, I surely will have no say in whom he picks to wed. I should be glad to see him settle with a woman of kindness and character."

Susan mulled over Lady Mayfield's words and their implications. Did her ladyship actually think the earl was attracted to her? Could such a match be possible? "I am not nobility," Susan blurted.

Her ladyship rose from her chair. She patted Susan's arm and said, "Neither was I thirty-two years ago. Goodnight, child," she said, and left Susan to her thoughts.

Ten

Arabella was barely awake when Peg arrived with the first present from Sir Richard—a large bouquet of tulips.

"Oh, my," said Susan, sitting up as Peg laid the offering on the bed. "What is this?"

"From Sir Richard." Peg handed over a card.

Arabella opened it and read, "Can you ever forgive me for so wrongly misjudging you?"

"He wants me to tell him if there is any message," said Peg.

Arabella sat, thoughtful. "Tell him there is no message."

Peg looked surprised, but took herself off.

Fifteen minutes later, she was back with the next offering—sticky buns from the bakery. This time the card read, "How can I bear it, knowing I have offended one so sweet?"

"Those look awful good," observed Peg as Arabella helped herself to one.

"They are," said Arabella, oblivious to the hint.

"Is there a message for Sir Richard?"

Arabella licked a finger and said, "No message."

The offerings continued throughout the morning; more flowers, a box of sweets from the confectioners, lacey handkerchiefs. At last, sensing the well would soon run dry, Arabella told Peg to inform Sir Richard that she might be under the apple tree that afternoon. "But first come help me dress."

"Will you wear your new gown?"

Arabella looked at the gown. She should show Sir Richard how little his presents meant, how very far above being bought she was. But she was sure she would look so much prettier in a nice gown. And she wanted Sir Richard to see just how pretty she was. "Yes, I think I will."

Lord Mayfield met the new day determined to unravel his confused thoughts and settle things with Arabella once and for all.

He was still sure he was participating in a farce written by his obnoxious ward. It had to be. Why else would the woman the girl claimed was her mother disavow any acquaintance with her? Arabella had, somehow, heard of this governess who looked like her and concocted the whole silly tale. He had to admit, it showed great ingenuity, and an amount of thought and planning of which he'd never have thought her capable.

But it was time to end the nonsense once and for all.

He told himself that what he was about to do was in no way related to the fact that the chit was beautiful and could actually, on occasion, make herself agreeable. He was *not* trying to prove to himself that she was someone other than Arabella. He was simply doing what any sensible man would do. He went to the library and wrote a note summoning a certain little man with sharp eyes and a talent for indistinctive dress to attend him at two o'clock. Next, he visited his mama in her sitting room.

His mother accepted his kiss and wish that she had slept well, then said, "And now, what is it you want Gerard?"

"I wondered when you plan next to pay morning calls."

"On whom do you wish me to call?"

The earl smiled. "I don't suppose Lady Wight is an intimate of yours."

"You are correct," said the countess. "She is an odious woman, entirely puffed up in her own conceit. Why would you wish to torture your mother so?"

"Lady Wight has or had a governess who looks much like Arabella. Cranston saw her."

"I see," said her ladyship, a smile teasing the corner of her mouth. "So this is to be some sort of test, rather like the princess and the pea?"

Her son made a face. "Really, Mother.

Must you put it quite like that? It is only one avenue I have decided to pursue in getting to the bottom of things. What I will, most likely, discover, is that Wight's cub is simply one more besotted fool whom Arabella has encouraged."

"Perhaps," said her ladyship.

"After all, the woman she claimed as mother denied any acquaintance with her."

"Very odd, indeed," said Lady Mayfield. "I wonder why a mother would do such a thing."

"She would have to be a very odd sort of mother to behave in such a fashion," said the earl.

Lady Mayfield smiled. "My son, don't you remember the story of Moses?"

"Moses!"

"Whose mother set him adrift in a little boat in the hopes that royalty would adopt him."

"I am hardly a pharaoh," snorted Mayfield. "And I have no intention of adopting the young lady."

"No. But you are an earl. And an unattached one at that."

Mayfield looked at his mother in amazement as the implications of what she was saying became clear. "You cannot be serious."

"It is a possibility that has occurred to me," said Lady Mayfield. "Our houseguest did write to her mother to tell her of her predicament. Perhaps the mother thought it would be in her daughter's best interests for her to remain under your roof."

"That is utterly crack-brained."

"That is mother love," observed her ladyship.

The earl merely shook his head before bringing them back to the subject at hand. "And speaking of mother love, will you call on Lady Wight?"

"It will be positively painful extricating myself from that woman's claws once she has them into me," predicted her ladyship. "You would make my life a great deal easier simply by hiring a Bow Street Runner to find your Arabella."

Now it was her son's turn to smile. "I am leaving no stone unturned, dearest, believe me."

Her ladyship sighed a martyr's sigh. "Very well, Gerard. I will do as you ask. It could prove amusing. I shall have to discover what day she is at home to visitors."

"Naturally," murmured Mayfield, and smiled. "You are a dear." He kissed her and went to the door.

"And Gerard."

"Yes, Mother?"

"While you are waiting for me to call on Lady Wight, why not send for Arabella's aunt? Surely she would know her own niece."

"An excellent suggestion," said the earl. "I don't know why I did not think of it myself."

"Possibly because your mind was so very occupied thinking ill of the young lady who is residing with us," said his mother sweetly, to which he made no reply.

Sir Richard was under the apple tree, starting his third mug of ale when he finally saw Arabella approaching. He hurried to take her hands in his. "You have forgiven me!" he cried, bowing humbly over them.

"I am not at all sure I should," she said.

"Oh, but you must. Else I will have no choice but to put an end to my existence."

"You must not do that," she said.

"But I shall. Unless you say you forgive me."

"Well," she hesitated.

"Say you forgive me now or I shall run into the street and throw myself under the wheels of the first carriage that comes by," he said. Arabella giggled and he smiled. "There now," he said. "Friends again?"

"Friends again," she agreed.

"Excellent," he said, leading her to the table. "Shall I fetch you some cider?" She shook her head and he sat down across from her. "You do, indeed, look incomparable in blue," he said and she lowered her gaze demurely. "And so much like a lady of quality that I am sure you must be exactly that."

She raised her eyes hopefully to his. "Oh, do you think so?"

AN INNOCENT IMPOSTER 171

"Well, I have been giving your situation much consideration. I thought about the valuable ring you showed me. And I remembered your hands."

"My hands?" She held them up and looked at them.

Sir Richard caught one. "They are lovely."

"Thank you," she murmured and blushed.

"And they are not the hands of a scullery maid."

"Why, how can you know?"

Sir Richard turned her hand palm up. "You have only to look at them to know. They are not roughened or red like they would be if you did menial labor." Gently, she extracted it and he continued, "You have the hands of a lady and you possess a valuable ring, but you were travelling in an inexpensive gown. All this can mean only one of two things. You are either a runaway lady's maid who has stolen from her mistress—"

Here Arabella gasped in horror.

"Hmmm," said Sir Richard, sounding like a doctor making a diagnosis. "The repugnance you just now showed convinces me that you cannot be a dishonest maid. So then, you can only be one thing."

"What is that?" asked Arabella, spellbound.

"Why, a lady of quality, of course," said Sir Richard.

Arabella clapped her hands. "Oh, yes! I

like that ever so much more than being a wicked servant. But why was I wearing such an ugly gown?"

"I was coming to that," said Sir Richard. He got up and began to pace, twirling the ribbon of his quizzing glass. "You were obviously running away."

Arabella's eyes grew wide.

"Now, why," continued Sir Richard, pointing his quizzing glass at her, "would a young lady of quality run away?"

She shook her head, at a loss.

"I'll wager it was from the prospect of a distasteful marriage."

"How horrible for me," said Arabella weakly. "And the ring?"

"Most likely, a present from your betrothed."

"If what you have just said is true, I had rather not ever be found," said Arabella miserably. "Perhaps even now he is looking for me."

Sir Richard stopped. "He! You said, 'he.' He who?"

Arabella squeezed her eyes shut in an effort to concentrate. "Oooh, I don't know," she moaned.

"Well, never mind," said Sir Richard. "And never fear. I will protect you."

She looked worshipfully up at him. "Oh, thank you. You are so very brave."

Sir Richard gave her a smile which said he wholeheartedly agreed with her.

AN INNOCENT IMPOSTER 173

"And so clever," she continued. "The way you figured out who I am was so very brilliant. I am sure I could never have done it."

Sir Richard, accepting her praise as his due, didn't bother with any modest disclaimers. "Now," he said, "if we could only learn your name. Does nothing come to mind?"

Arabella shook her head.

Sir Richard rubbed his chin. "Perhaps we are going about this in the wrong way," he said after a moment. "Let's try this. We will pretend that"— he ran to where she sat and pulled her to her feet— "you have been in Hatchard's and purchased a book."

"What sort of book."

"What sort of . . . ? well, I daresay it don't matter. Just something or other."

"But how can I pretend I am in a book store when I don't even know what sort of book I am purchasing?"

"True," conceded Sir Richard. "What sort of book do you like to read."

"Oh, dear," Arabella sighed, heartily discouraged. "I cannot even remember what sort of book I like to read. How will I ever be able to remember my name?"

"Perhaps you cannot remember what sort of book you like to read because you are not bookish," said Sir Richard. "So we shan't worry about it. Let us just say you have come in search of Caro Lamb's novel, for everyone is reading that."

"Are they? I should like to know what it

is about if everyone is reading it," said Arabella eagerly.

"And so you shall," said Sir Richard, refusing to be sidetracked further, "as soon as you have taken it home and read it. Now. You stand here. I will pretend to open the door. You look up and I will say, "Good morning, Miss— and you supply the name."

"What shall we do if I can think of no name?" asked Arabella, panicked. "I cannot even now think of one."

"You mustn't overtax your mind trying to think of a name now," said Sir Richard. "That will defeat our purpose. You must say the first name that comes into your head, don't you see? That is how we will know it is yours. Whatever comes naturally to mind must be the name that belongs to you."

"I suppose," said Arabella doubtfully.

Sir Richard took a few steps away from her. "All right, then. Are you ready to try?" She nodded and he opened an imaginary door and strode toward her, allowing himself to nearly bump into her. "Oh, pardon me. Why, I do believe it is Miss . . ."

"Lay . . ." she began.

"Yes, yes," he urged.

"Lay . . . Layne!" she exclaimed. "That name sounds familiar."

Sir Richard slapped his hands together. "Now we are getting somewhere. Miss Layne?"

"Oh, yes." Arabella nodded eagerly. "I

AN INNOCENT IMPOSTER

know I have heard that name before. It must be mine."

"Excellent," said Sir Richard, rubbing his hands together.

"Now what should we do?" asked Arabella.

Sir Richard scratched his head. "Let me think. We must discover why you were running away." He paced some more, deep in thought. "I have it! I shall place an advertisement in the *Gazette*. We will find your family and discover the mystery behind that ring all at once."

"But what sort of advertisement?"

"I know just the thing," said Sir Richard, taking her by the hand and leading her back into the inn. "We will just seek out pen and paper."

Ten minutes later Sir Richard tipped back in his chair in the private dining room and read the results of their combined efforts aloud, " 'This is to inform the possessor of a certain ring that he may get in touch with Miss Layne in care of The Swan, Reigate.' Now. I shall go to London and place this advertisement myself."

"You must leave me all alone here?"

"I shan't be gone long," said Sir Richard gently. He studied her face, then asked, "Will you miss me?"

She didn't answer. Instead, she said, "I am afraid I have monopolized a great deal of your time."

"I have enjoyed every minute of it."

She smiled at this. But then worry took over and she fretted, "Oh, I do hope your idea works. I am beginning to feel rather like an orphan, unloved and unwanted."

"Never say such a thing," said Sir Richard. "For you could never be unloved."

Arabella lowered her gaze, suddenly feeling unaccountably shy.

The dandy bit his lip and regarded her longingly. At last he said, "I know I have no right to speak. Not until we discover who you are."

"I understand," said Arabella in a small voice. "I may prove to be unworthy of your regard." This thought was so painful her throat constricted and she was barely able to get out the words.

"Unworthy!" he cried. "It is I who is unworthy. It is my fault you are at this inn with no memory of who you are. I don't deserve your slightest regard."

"You mustn't say such a thing," scolded Arabella.

"I am not a wealthy man," confessed Sir Richard.

Arabella shrugged. Suddenly fine gowns and presents did not matter so very much. If she had to choose between such things and keeping Sir Richard she would definitely choose him. But he had to marry for money. "We may discover that I am not a wealthy woman," she said.

AN INNOCENT IMPOSTER 177

He laughed bitterly. "Then we would be in a fix."

Arabella bit her thumb. "I suppose you would not wish to marry me if were a poor woman," she said at last.

Sir Richard was instantly on his knees before her. He took her hand and kissed it. "There is no woman on earth I would rather have. But I am . . . Oh, my dear Miss Layne, I am not at all worthy of you. Nonetheless, would you marry me?"

Arabella blushed and nodded. "If I am able."

With hope thus planted in his heart, Sir Richard set off for London early the following morning.

When she finally awoke, Arabella learned from Peg that he had already gone. Without Sir Richard there to see her, she decided there was no sense in wearing her fine new gown, so she had Peg help her into the old one. Her arm was feeling better, and she decided to do without the trussing, which was a terrible nuisance and didn't look at all pretty. Holding her arm, she went downstairs, wondering what she would do to while away the time in Sir Richard's absence. It was a lovely day. Perhaps she would take a little walk.

She was about to go out the door when Mrs. Dickens waylaid her. "Well, missy. Your fine gentleman has gone off without paying his shot, nor yours for the week to come."

"He has only gone to London to place an advertisement in the *Gazette*," said Arabella. "He will be back in three days' time."

"So you say," said Mrs. Dickens. "But I have only your word for it, and for all I know the fellow has tricked you as well as meself."

"Oh, no. I can assure you he will return," said Arabella earnestly.

"Well, we can hope," said Mrs. Dickens. "Meanwhile there is the bill to pay."

"But I am sure Sir Richard will pay as soon as he returns."

"Until he returns, Miss High-and-Mighty, you had best find some ways to make yourself useful."

It was at that moment that Arabella noticed the sudsy bucket in Mrs. Dickens' hand. Her eyes grew wide. "Oh, you cannot think to make me—"

Mrs. Dickens shoved the bucket at her, and a scrub brush as well. "I can," she said. "Start here in the entryway."

"But I know nothing of scrubbing floors," protested Arabella.

"Anyone can scrub a floor. Even you," replied Mrs. Dickens. She turned and waddled off down the hallway, calling over her shoulder, "And tonight you can help Peg serve in the taproom."

The taproom! What sort of female did that woman think her? Arabella fell to her knees beside the sudsy bucket, tears of self

AN INNOCENT IMPOSTER 179

pity giving her a watery view of the floor. She took the scrub brush and dipped it in the water and received a fresh shock. With a yelp, she yanked out her scalded hand. This was the last straw! She burst into noisy wails.

"Oh, miss!" She was vaguely aware of Peg kneeling beside her. "What are you doing here?"

"Mrs. Dickens has set me to work cleaning the floor and I don't know how," sobbed Arabella.

Peg clucked her tongue. "The shame of it. Making a fine lady like you do such a thing."

"Do you really think I am a fine lady?" asked Arabella hopefully.

"Gracious, yes! Else you wouldn't be sitting here crying because you had to scrub the floor." Peg looked over her shoulder. "Here. You go on now. I'll do this."

"Oh, but Peg. She will catch you and you will get into trouble."

Peg shook her head. "She'll be busy in the kitchen the next hour. I can have this done in two shakes of a lamb's tail."

"But don't you have other work to do?" protested Arabella.

"You never mind me, miss. I can get my work done."

"Oh, thank you, Peg!" Arabella hugged her rescuer. She handed over the scrub brush, got up and bolted out the front door to freedom.

She did not have such a lucky escape that night, however. Mrs. Dickens found her and hauled her off to the taproom.

"But my arm," protested Arabella. "I cannot carry heavy mugs with a sore arm."

"Carry them with the one that is good," said Mrs. Dickens in disgust. "Really, I never met such a lazy girl in all my born days."

Arabella looked at her in shock. Surely no one had ever talked to her in such a way. Had they?

"Now get over to Mr. Dickens and get busy. We have a house full of thirsty men."

Arabella looked nervously about the taproom. It was hazy with pipe smoke. Through the haze she could see a crowd of men, clustered about the tables in groups. Raucous laughter erupted from various parts of the room, making her even more uncomfortable than the smell of unwashed bodies.

"Go on now," said Mrs. Dickens, giving her a push.

Slowly, she made her way to the bar where Mr. Dickens was filling pewter mugs with ale and porter. Peg hurried past her, three tall mugs in each hand, and gave her an encouraging smile.

"Here you are," he said, as soon as she got within hearing distance. "I've got three ales to go to the corner table on the far side of the hearth."

Arabella swallowed, took two mugs with her good hand and managed to get the other one in spite of her sore arm, then made her way to the far table, where three red-faced, hefty men sat. They smiled at her as if she were a Christmas present and their warm welcome did nothing to make her feel any better about this task Mrs. Dickens had set her. Nervously, she set the mugs on the scarred table.

"Well, now, what's this," said the nearest man, wrapping an arm around her hips and drawing her next to him. "Someone new?"

"Let me go!" she commanded, shocked.

"Oh, not friendly, eh?" teased the man. "Well, you can't set down drinks for a man and not be a little friendly," he said, giving her a squeeze.

"Stop!" she cried.

The man laughed and set her free, and when she turned to leave, gave her a swat on the bottom.

Arabella's eyes opened in shock and she put a horrified hand to her mouth. This produced guffaws from, not only the men at the table, but a host of others sitting nearby. Horror and shame reduced her to tears and she ran from the room, the men's laughter pursuing her.

She didn't stop running until she'd gotten to her room. Once inside, she locked the door and pulled a chair in front of it for good measure. She might not remember who, exactly, she was, but she knew for certain she was not a serving wench! Arabella sighed. Which meant that, tomorrow she would, most likely, be back to peeling potatoes.

The next three days Susan noticed a change in the earl. He seemed to avoid her as much as possible, but when circumstances brought them together he was formal and polite. It seemed as if he were forcing himself to hold to some sort of truce. He said nothing to bait or antagonize her, and on more than one occasion she had caught him observing her, a thoughtful expression on his face. Was he, perhaps, beginning to believe her?

It was a Tuesday when Lady Mayfield sent word to Susan that they would be making morning calls, instructing her to please be ready at one o'clock. She supposed that paying social calls was preferable to sitting about wondering what the earl was thinking, and shortly after one she followed the countess into the Mayfield landau.

Susan didn't recognize the house they stopped in front of, and so waited in the carriage in ignorance while the earl's footman went to knock on the door and deliver Lady Mayfield's calling card.

She remained in that happy state until they had mounted the steps and got inside. Susan clutched Lady Mayfield's arm. "Your ladyship, I am feeling unwell," she whis-

AN INNOCENT IMPOSTER

pered, trying to avoid the butler's shocked stare.

Her Ladyship pried Susan's hand from her arm and said, "I am sure you will be fine if you can but sit down."

Susan swallowed and followed the countess into the drawing room, where she found herself face to face with her former employer.

The smile on Lady Wight's boney face shrank to nothing and that woman's eyes grew to enormous proportions. She managed to recover enough to say in a faint voice, "How very kind of you to call, Lady Mayfield."

Her ladyship took a seat opposite Lady Wight. "I don't believe you have met my son's ward, Miss Arabella Leighton."

"Leighton?" managed Lady Wight. "But this cannot be."

"What cannot be?" asked Lady Mayfield, looking innocently from her pale faced companion to Lady Wight.

"This young woman is your son's ward, you say?"

"Why, yes. Does she look familiar to you?"

"I do beg your pardon, my dear," gushed Lady Wight to Susan, "but you look remarkably like . . . that is, you bear a distinct resemblance to another young woman of my acquaintance."

"Isn't that amazing!" declared Lady Mayfield. "And what is her name?"

"Oh, I am sure you would not know her," said Lady Wight. "Her name was Layne."

"Layne," said Lady Mayfield. She seemed to consider this, then turned to the mute Susan and asked, "Do you, perhaps, have cousins by that name my dear?"

"I might," managed Susan.

"Oh, I am sure you are not in the least related," said Lady Wight. "This young woman had no connections. She was governess to my daughter. *Before* I caught her setting her cap for my son. I dismissed the creature before we came to town." Her ladyship gave a satisfied nod. "I imagine she is back in Crawley, wishing she had behaved with more propriety."

Susan caught herself making a face of disgust and wiped it off. She looked to see if Lady Mayfield had seen her. Lady Mayfield was biting back a smile.

Eleven

Lady Mayfield found her son in the library and reported to him the details of her visit to Lady Wight. "I wish you had been there, Gerard. The woman looked as though I had brought a scullery maid to call. No, worse— a traitor to the crown at the very least. The resemblance between these girls must truly be remarkable."

"And Arabella?"

"Turned white as a ghost when she first saw her. Of course, the sight of Lady Wight is enough to frighten anyone, I vow. Such a scarecrow of a woman."

"So Arabella turned white," prompted the earl.

"When she realized where we were, she clutched my arm until I thought it would go numb. She obviously is acquainted with Lady Wight and has had unpleasant dealings with her."

"And what did Arabella say after you left?"

"Why, she said she hoped she had not embarrassed me. Rather a considerate statement for such a spoilt child, I must say."

Mayfield frowned.

"The story Lady Wight told was the same one our guest has insisted on," continued Lady Mayfield. "Miss Susan Layne was governess to the Earl of Wight's daughter at his country seat. The girl was dismissed and sent home to Crawley shortly before the Wight's came to town."

The earl got up and began to pace.

"Gerard, what is it?" asked his mama.

"I had the opportunity to read today's *Gazette* while you were out visiting." He picked the paper from his desk and passed it to his mother, indicating the part he wished her to read.

"Ring . . . Miss Layne . . . I don't understand."

"Nor do I," said the earl. He rubbed his chin. What *was* that thought that kept nibbling at the back of his brain? Alice! "She called the woman Alice!" he declared with a snap of the fingers.

"What woman? Gerard, what are you talking about?"

"When we went to Crawley. That woman said, 'Alice, fetch the hartshorn' . . . or some such thing. But Arabella called the maid Alice."

"What is so remarkable in that? It is probably the girl's name."

"And Arabella knew it! How could she

know the maid's name unless she was who she's always claimed to be?"

At that moment there was a knock at the library door and Miss Layne, herself, made an appearance. "I have received a letter in today's post. I thought your lordship should read it."

She held out the missive and the earl took it, and read, " 'My dear daughter,

" 'By now I imagine you are engaged and I feel safe in writing to you.' " Here the earl looked up in amazement at Susan, whose pink cheeks were deepening in color. He returned his attention to the letter and continued, " 'I pray you will forgive your poor mama for embarrassing you so when you came to call. But what mother, when presented such an opportunity to see her daughter securely married would do otherwise?' I can hardly credit it," he said.

"Is there more?" prompted Lady Mayfield.

"Oh, yes, there is more. 'I know you will be very happy, dearest, as you deserve to be. You can be sure that our little sitting room was full to overflowing as soon as the rains let up, and there is not a person in all of Crawley, I can assure you, Susan dearest, who is not thrilled with your good fortune. I am sure the Earl of Mayfield will understand a mother's heart and forgive my little deception—' *Little* deception? She calls this a little deception? I should hate to see her idea of any greater trickery!"

"Gerard. You are shouting," scolded Lady Mayfield.

The earl rubbed his forehead. "Forgive me." He turned his attention to Susan, who was now seated and looking at her lap. "Miss Layne," he began. "It seems so odd to call you that, since I have, all this time thought of you as Arabella." She was sitting still as stone and he bit his lip. "It would appear I have been very wrong and owe you a great apology."

If the earl thought this would comfort her, he was wrong, for she covered her face and burst into tears. He looked to his mother for help, but she merely shrugged, putting responsibility for comforting the lady squarely back on his shoulders. He pulled out a Belcher handkerchief and knelt before her, trying to insert it between her hands. "Here now, there is no need to weep. Things will be sorted out soon." This statement seemed to have little comforting effect. "Miss Layne, please. You must get hold of yourself."

She took a great gulp of air and came to a sobbing stop.

"There now," said the earl gently. "Dry your eyes, and I shall show you something in the *Gazette* which might interest you." She obeyed and the earl took the paper from his mother and presented it to her. She read it then looked at him, shaking her head. "I don't understand," she said.

"Neither do I, precisely. But I believe if I

go to The Swan in Reigate I will find the answer to a great many questions."

"An excellent idea, Gerard," said her ladyship. "I should fancy a drive to Reigate. We must leave first thing tomorrow."

"*I* must leave immediately," said Mayfield. "Now, Gerard, you shan't exclude either Miss Layne or me from this adventure. After all we have both been involved from the start. Miss Layne, especially, deserves to come along."

The earl looked none too happy about this. "Mother, it will be a long drive. I shan't stop but to change horses."

"We won't mind, will we, my dear?"

"I am a good traveler," said Susan.

"Very well," he said. "But we shan't wait until tomorrow. We leave in half an hour."

"Excellent," said her ladyship. "I am quite looking forward to seeing Miss Layne's mirror image. We can all dine together at The Swan tonight." She smiled broadly. "I understand they serve an excellent humble pie."

Her son watched her leave the room and scowled. Miss Layne rose to follow her. "Miss Layne," he said.

She stopped, not looking back. "Yes, your lordship?" she said in a small voice.

"I truly am sorry for the many misunderstandings we have had. I hope you will allow me to make up for the grief and embarrassment I have caused you."

"I am sure it was an easy enough mistake

to make," she replied. "I am aware that your ward and I look greatly alike, and you were certainly not the only person to mistake my identity."

"I was utterly pig headed," said Mayfield, feeling the fool afresh. And what the devil could he do about it? Inspiration hit. "I hope you will accept the gowns you have worn as a present for all the trouble my family has caused you. And I know my mother will be happy to write a reference for you."

"Your lordship is most kind," she said coldly and left him without another word.

That had been a dunderheaded thing to do! He should have written her a voucher. No. She would have been as insulted by that as she was by his offer just now. He had to make a grander gesture. But what else could he do for the girl?

Of course! He would offer her a London season. Someone was bound to want her, even if she had neither title nor fortune. She was gently bred, she was beautiful.

He sighed and wished that Miss Layne wasn't a governess and that they'd met under different circumstances.

The Earl of Redburrough extended his large legs and tried to stretch the stiffness from them. The carriage was becoming increasingly confining, and he was glad he had instructed his coachman to stop at The

AN INNOCENT IMPOSTER

Swan. He was ready for a meal and a chance to move about. He would spend the night at the inn, then get an early start for London in the morning. He would call on Miss Leighton the very next day.

The earl smiled at the thought of seeing that pretty young lady again. Such a little minx! She would be a breath of fresh air in his life, a welcome distraction from the tedium of estate business.

He did wonder how well she would take to country life. Well, she would simply have to adjust, for Redburrough had no intention of spending every spring in London, dashing about to balls and routs and heaven knew what else.

Besides, once she saw Redburrough Hall, Miss Leighton would never want to leave it. Heaven only knew any number of young ladies had dropped broad hints about how very much they would enjoy life at the hall.

Miss Leighton had been the loveliest of them all, and she would grace his home beautifully. He could hardly wait to see the Redburrough rubies hanging around that pretty white neck and dropping from her ears. He closed his eyes and imagined Miss Leighton clad only in the Redburrough rubies, and enjoyed a lecherous chuckle. An excellent idea. He must remember it.

Sir Richard and Arabella were returning to The Swan from a stroll to St. Mary Magdalene's Church when the coach from London arrived. They stood and watched the passengers descend.

"Does anyone look familiar to you?" asked Sir Richard.

Arabella shook her head. "I am afraid not."

She looked at him sadly and he patted her hand. "Don't worry. Someone is bound to show up soon."

She smiled and nodded and they turned to go inside the inn. That was when she caught sight of the little man with the dark hair and the rather cheap looking coat following behind them. She took a tighter hold on Sir Richard's arm.

"What is it?" he asked.

"There is an odd little man behind us, who was looking at me most curiously."

Sir Richard looked over his shoulder and saw a short man strolling off in the direction of the coachman.

"Do you see him?" asked Arabella.

"Yes, but you must have imagined his interest in us," replied Sir Richard, "for he has gone off to talk with the coachman."

"I suppose this waiting is having its effects on my nerves," she said.

"We shall have some cider and you will feel much better," Sir Richard predicted. "Would you care to take it under the apple tree."

"Oh, yes," she said.

AN INNOCENT IMPOSTER

"I shall fetch it and meet you there directly."

Sir Richard went off in search of cider and Arabella made her way to the shady little garden with the apple tree. She was sure someone was watching her, but when she turned she saw no one.

She was glad when Sir Richard finally joined her. "My, but it took you a long time," she observed.

"Dickens is up to his elbows in customers just now." Sir Richard grinned. "And Mrs. Dickens stopped me, wondering where you were."

Arabella made a face. "I can well imagine why. Did she think I should like to help her serve food to the travelers with one arm?"

"She can think all she likes, but I shan't allow her to work you any more. Never fear."

"You have been so very good to me," said Arabella.

"And I hope to spend the rest of my life doing so," said Sir Richard.

They managed to while away the rest of the afternoon in the garden, and finally Sir Richard suggested they go in. "It is getting chilly."

"I do believe you are right," said Arabella, repeating a phrase that was coming much into use lately.

They rose and he gave her his arm. As they made their way toward the inn Arabella was sure she caught sight of the same little man she'd seen earlier. "There is that man again! He just went around the corner of the inn."

"My dear, I am sure you are imagining things," said Sir Richard.

"No, I am not," she insisted. "I saw him. Just now."

"Well, we will keep our eyes open for him," said Sir Richard. "Just remember he cannot hurt you while I am with you. Now. Are you hungry? I must confess this country air gives me a horse's appetite."

"If you care to eat now I shall bear you company," said Arabella. "I'll just go take off my new bonnet," she added, smiling at him. "I really should not have allowed you to purchase it for me."

"You could hardly continue to wear that other thing," said Sir Richard. "It was positively dowdy, all crushed and dirtied as it was."

"You will spoil me."

"Impossible."

Arabella blushed and said, "I'll only be a moment."

"See that you are, for I cannot go long without your company," said Sir Richard. He watched her go up the stairs, enjoying a glimpse of delicate ankle as she went, then wandered off to the dining room to secure a table.

The room was full of travelers, and Sir Richard would have preferred to dine with

AN INNOCENT IMPOSTER

Miss Layne alone, far from the eyes of strangers, but love had burdened him with a strong sense of propriety and he wasn't anxious to put the lady in any more of a compromising situation than she already was. He found a table in the corner of the room by a window.

He caught sight of the same little man they had seen outside and realized the man was looking at him, but as soon as the man realized Sir Richard had noticed him he glanced away. Sir Richard's eyes narrowed and he scrutinized the little man, who was now taking tea and pretending great absorption with the process. Bow Street Runner, undoubtedly. Why the devil was the man watching him? Or was it Miss Layne he was watching? Sir Richard got up from his seat and ambled over to his table.

The man looked up at him in feigned surprise.

"I believe you have been watching me, sir, and I should like to know why," said Sir Richard.

"I am sorry. You are mistaken," said the little man, and he started to rise.

Sir Richard put a hand to his shoulder and forced him back into his seat. "You would oblige me by telling me for whom you are looking."

"I am sorry, sir, but I really am afraid you have made a mistake," said the little man.

"I am merely a traveler on my way to Brighton."

"Yes, and I am the Prince Regent," said Sir Richard casually. He tightened his grip on the man's shoulder. "Who hired you?"

At that moment, Arabella made her appearance in the dining room and the man's eyes widened at the sight of her. Sir Richard followed his gaze. "Do you know that young lady?"

"I have never met her before," said the man.

Sir Richard grabbed his cravat. "Don't lie to me, fellow."

"It is true. I swear it."

Arabella came running up to stand beside Sir Richard. "I was right. He was following us."

"Who hired you?" demanded Sir Richard. The man remained stubbornly silent and Sir Richard gave his cravat a yank, pulling him from his seat. "Tell me now or I shall have to slit your gullet."

"Mayfield," croaked the man. "The Earl of Mayfield."

Sir Richard let go of the man's cravat and he fell back onto his seat and rubbed his neck.

"The Earl of Mayfield," repeated Sir Richard, turning to Arabella. "Does that name mean something to you, my dear?"

"Mayfield. Oh," said Arabella in a shaky voice. "It does sound very familiar. But I confess, hearing it does not make me feel at all comfortable. I am not sure what my relationship with the man can be."

The little man scowled. "He is your guardian," he said.

Sir Richard was suddenly aware of several pairs of eyes on them. "I think, perhaps, this conversation would be best continued in the private parlor. Come, sir. I shall buy you your dinner. It is the least I can do after the rough treatment I gave you just now."

The little man dusted off his coat and adjusted his cravat, then with as much pride as a man who has nearly been publicly strangled can muster, preceded Sir Richard from the room. The three repaired to a private room and Sir Richard shut the door. "Now," he said, "perhaps you can tell us why the Earl of Mayfield sent you here." Sir Richard indicated a seat at the table.

The little man took it. "The earl hired me to come to this inn and search for a young woman with yaller curls and blue eyes. He said she was very beautiful and there was no mistaking her. I was to see if she was well and who she was with and then let him know."

"Why did he not come look for her himself?" demanded Sir Richard.

"He didn't say," replied the little man stiffly.

"A fine guardian," scoffed Sir Richard. He turned to Arabella, who had seated herself opposite the stranger. "You were, most likely running away from him. I hope he did not beat you. I shan't be responsible for what I may have to do to him if I discover he beat you."

At that moment Mr. Dickens entered the room, fussing and babbling to a large man with two chins and salt and pepper hair.

"What the devil are you about, Dickens," began Sir Richard irritably. But curiosity stopped him from demanding the landlord take the encroaching newcomer off to the public dining room. "Lord Redburrough, is it not?"

Arabella's brows furrowed. "Redburrough?" She turned in her seat to look at the newcomer. Her eyes widened. "Redburrough?" she repeated.

"Oh, so you all know each other," said Dickens, relieved. "Then perhaps your lordship wouldn't mind sharing the room—"

Lord Redburrough stopped in the middle of the room and pushed Mr. Dickens aside. He stared at Arabella, disbelief and anger mingling on his face. "Miss Leighton?"

Sir Richard looked at Arabella questioningly. "Miss Leighton?"

Redburrough was at their table in three giant strides. "Miss Leighton. Why do I find

AN INNOCENT IMPOSTER 199

you here?" He scowled at Sir Richard and added, "Where is your guardian?"

"Oh, my. I am . . ." Arabella's eyes rolled back and she slumped in her chair in a faint.

Twelve

As Lord Mayfield climbed out of his carriage at The Swan, he noticed another crested carriage. Once he had helped his mother and Susan down, he nodded to it and said, "This will bring things to a head quickly, I'll warrant."

Susan looked inquisitively at Lady Mayfield, who said, "Redburrough's carriage."

The three were barely inside the inn when a fat man with a red nose came striding down the hall, bellowing, "Mrs. Dickens!" He stopped short at the sight of the earl's party and his mouth gaped open. "Oh, Lordy," he muttered, then bowed as low as his belly would allow. "Welcome, your grace, to The Swan. I am so sorry I wasn't at the door to greet you properly."

"Your lordship will do," said Mayfield. "I see we arrive at an inconvenient time."

"No, no," said the man quickly. "Not in the least. I am, however, sorry to have to inform your lordship that our private parlor is bespoken."

AN INNOCENT IMPOSTER 201

The sound of raised voices emanated from the parlor.

"Rather vociferously so, it would appear," observed Mayfield.

"Just a bit of a misunderstanding," said Mr. Dickens uneasily.

"Have you any rooms?" asked Mayfield.

"Oh, yes, yes. We have excellent rooms." At that moment an enormous woman with a gravy spattered apron stretched across her great girth came waddling into sight. "Ah, my dear," said the landlord. "I was just now looking for you. The young lady in the private parlor has fainted and there is great commotion."

"If it is the young lady I think it is," replied his wife, "she may wait until we are finished seeing to this fine gentleman's needs." She smiled at the earl and gave a curtsey that made her body roll like the swell of the wave.

"You have a young guest giving you trouble?" asked the earl in conversational tones. His sympathetic face encouraged the sharing of confidences.

Mrs. Dickens rolled her eyes. "Your lordship wouldn't believe the half of it. Some poor young woman was throwed from the Eclipse three weeks ago and has no memory of who she is."

"How fortunate that I have arrived to tell her," said Mayfield. "Where is she?"

Mrs. Dickens' little currant eyes opened to

grape proportions and she pointed down the hallway to the private parlor.

The three travelers hurried down the hall and arrived at the door in time to witness Lord Redburrough informing Miss Arabella Leighton that she had played fast and loose with him.

Sir Richard, who was half the older man's size let out a growl and shoved a fist into Lord Redburrough's jaw, sending him flying backwards.

The young lady, now very much out of her faint, cried out Sir Richard's name as if she feared for his life.

Sir Richard, however, didn't hear her. He stood over the fallen Lord Redburrough, ready to pummel him again as soon as he was up.

The little man whom the earl had hired to find his ward was standing nearby, a perplexed expression on his face.

With an effort, Lord Mayfield held back the guffaw that had worked its way up from his belly to his throat. He motioned for the ladies to wait in the hallway and entered the room. "Well, now. What have we here?"

Arabella looked up and gave a gasp. "Barrymore!"

Sir Richard was momentarily distracted from Lord Redburrough, who was moaning and rubbing his jaw. "Barrymore? Do you know this man, my dear?"

"Yer lordship," managed the little man.

AN INNOCENT IMPOSTER

"I see you have found my missing ward, Mr. Williams. I am in your debt," said the earl.

"She was keeping company with this gentleman," said the little man, indicating Sir Richard.

The earl raised an inquiring eyebrow. "And you, sir, are?"

Sir Richard bowed politely. "Sir Richard Gaine, at your service, my lord. And you must be—"

"I am Mayfield."

By now Lord Redburrough had picked himself up from the floor. "A fine way you have of watching over your ward, Mayfield. I stop here for the night and find her with this . . . fellow."

"I am not a fellow," replied Sir Richard hotly. "I am Sir Richard Gaine."

"And you have been watching over the lady?" put in Mayfield.

This caused the Earl of Redburrough to grind his teeth and move in Gaine's direction.

Lord Mayfield put out a staying arm. "You see, Redburrough, it was necessary for someone to care for her. She was in a carriage accident and lost all memory of who she was. Is that not correct, my dear?"

Arabella was looking from one man to the other, as if trying to learn more about herself. "It is true I have had no memory of who I was or why I was here," she said.

"You ran away," Mayfield informed her.

"Ran away!" spluttered Redburrough. "You allowed the girl to run away and stay at this inn for who knows how long with this jackanapes?"

Sir Richard looked like a horse gone mad. "Pray, lend me your glove, sir."

"I shall do nothing of the sort," said Mayfield. "A duel is all that is lacking to make this whole ridiculous matter even more of a scandal than it already appears." He turned to Lord Redburrough. "I am sorry, Redburrough. My ward changed her mind about marrying you and I foolishly thought to force her into it."

"Changed her mind?" Lord Redburrough was incredulous. He turned to Arabella. "Never say that is why you ran away."

"I suppose it must be," she said. She turned to Lord Mayfield. "You must have been a most odious guardian if you drove me to run away."

"I must have," agreed Mayfield amiably. He turned back to Redburrough. "At any rate, I came after her immediately. And found her, too. Or so I thought."

"What drivel are you telling me?" demanded Redburrough.

"I am telling you that I brought back the wrong female."

"Such nonsense! For what sort of fool do you take me?"

AN INNOCENT IMPOSTER 205

"I will let you be the judge," said Mayfield, and called, "Miss Layne."

"Miss Layne?" echoed Arabella, and looked questioningly at Sir Richard, who regarded her in turn, equally puzzled.

Through the door walked the mirror image of Arabella Leighton, followed by Lady Mayfield.

"My God," said Redburrough.

"Why, she looks just like me," said Arabella. She cocked her head to the side. "Even the pelisse she is wearing looks familiar." Her eyes narrowed suspiciously. "So does the bonnet."

"Miss Layne has been wearing your clothes," admitted the earl.

"While I have been here peeling potatoes?"

"Peeling potatoes?" echoed Mayfield gleefully.

Neither young lady paid him the least attention. "Did you not get my letter?" asked Susan.

"What letter?"

"I wrote you a letter care of this inn, telling you that your guardian had mistaken me for you. I tried to tell him who I was, but he insisted I was you, playing a trick on him, and he forced me to return to London with him."

Arabella was still studying Susan. "How very strange," she said. "I feel as if I am looking into a mirror. Of course, your mouth is wider than mine," she added critically.

"Never mind that," said Redburrough. "What of our engagement? That is what I want to know."

"If the lady ran away simply to escape it, I should say it is at an end," put in Sir Richard.

"Now, look here young scoundrel," growled Lord Redburrough.

"Now, Redburrough," put in Mayfield placatingly.

"Take your hand off me, Mayfield. This entire situation is your fault. I hold you personally responsible."

"I hold myself responsible," said Lord Mayfield humbly. "I certainly managed to make a botch of things." He led the earl a ways away from the others. "But you can see how she is," he continued in a low voice. "Look at all the trouble the chit has caused me and then think of what a hell she would make your life if you married her."

"*I* should know how to handle her," said Redburrough.

"Indeed, I am sure you would. But what a nuisance! How much better to find yourself a biddable female who won't always be running off, getting in accidents and losing her memory. God knows what sort of damage that fall did to the girl's mind. Why, it may be years before we see the full extent of it."

AN INNOCENT IMPOSTER 207

Lord Redburrough looked thoughtful. "You have a point there," he said. "Well, if the child wishes to cry off, I'll not stand in her way. After all, there's no real harm done, I suppose. I did tell m' sister . . ."

"If I were you I should write to your sister and tell her you have had a narrow escape," advised Mayfield.

"Yes, yes. Not bad advice, Mayfield. Well, then," Lord Redburrough boomed, turning about and moving toward Arabella. "It seems to me that, perhaps, you are right, Miss Leighton. We should not suit." He stood as if waiting for something.

"I believe you have a ruby ring belonging to the earl," prompted Mayfield.

"Oh, is that whom it belongs to?" asked Arabella, and surprised the earl by removing the ring and handing it to Redburrough without the slightest fuss. "I am sorry I did not wish to marry you," she said politely.

Redburrough bowed stiffly.

"Well," said Mayfield, "now I believe we may all make use of this room and order some dinner."

"If you will excuse me, I think I shall press on toward London," said Lord Redburrough.

Mayfield looked properly disappointed. "Of course. Let me just accompany you to your carriage."

The little man, who had been standing about trying to look as if he were paying no attention to what was happening cleared his throat. "If your lordship don't mind, I think I'll take myself off as well."

"Yes, of course. Good job, Williams. You will have my check day after tomorrow," said the earl.

The little man bowed, thanked him, and left, and as the earl and Lord Redburrough followed him out, Lord Mayfield could again be heard apologizing for the way he had mishandled his ward's affairs.

"No wonder the sight of that ring made you so unhappy," observed Sir Richard.

"You are acquainted with that man?" asked Arabella.

"I know him more by reputation than acquaintance. Brutal to his cattle." Sir Richard shook his head. "If a man can treat his horses so, God knows how he would treat a wife."

Arabella heaved a sigh of relief. "I shall be eternally grateful to you for delivering me from marriage to him."

Sir Richard caught her hand to his lips and kissed it reverently. "I shall spend my entire life atoning for the terrible injury I caused you."

Lady Mayfield now deemed it time to step forward. "So this is the real Arabella," she said. "I am glad to meet you at last."

"Should I remember you?" asked Arabella.

Her ladyship smiled. "I can assure you, my

dear, had you met me you would have had good cause to remember me. I am Lady Mayfield. It would appear that as soon as my son has given his blessing I may wish you both happy."

The couple smiled at Lady Mayfield, then at each other. Everyone in the room, in fact, was now smiling, although Miss Layne's smile never quite reached her eyes.

Mayfield returned to the room, followed shortly after by Peg, all agog and carrying a stack of plates. Mrs. Dickens made her appearance soon after Peg, bearing a platter piled high with thick slices of beef. This was followed by a bowl of roast potatoes, green peas, and steak and kidney pie. With each entrance, Mrs. Dickens' face showed plainly what she thought of the way Providence rewarded lazy and spoilt young women.

The table was at last laid, and the party sat down to dine. The meal was made lively by Arabella's account of her adventures at the inn, all except her horrible experience in the taproom, which was entirely too mortifying to relate.

"We shan't pay her a farthing, my love," said Sir Richard when she had finished. "That will teach the woman to take advantage of ladies who have lost their memories."

"My love?" said Mayfield softly, and Sir Richard flushed.

After they had dined, the earl suggested the two gentlemen take a walk. "You are fond of my ward?" he asked as they sauntered out of the inn.

"I adore her," said Sir Richard fervently. He bit his lip, wrestling with a dilemma.

The earl waited.

At last Sir Richard said, "You had best hear it now. It was my fault Miss Leighton was injured. I was the one holding the ribbons of the coach when the accident occurred."

"Foxed, eh?"

Sir Richard's face took on a ruddy hue. He lowered his gaze and nodded.

"Well," said Mayfield, "you aren't the first man to overturn a coach, and I daresay you won't be the last."

"I have no money," blurted Sir Richard.

Mayfield looked at him in amazement. "None?"

"Not a feather to fly with."

The earl's first thought was to tell Sir Richard he was deeply sorry, but he couldn't allow his ward to marry a man with no money. How could he let his old friend's daughter to marry such a scamp?

On the other hand, how, when life was offering to teach Arabella about love and sacrifice, could he refuse the offer? He grinned. "Don't let it worry you," he said. "Arabella has more than enough."

"Arabella." Sir Richard's brow furrowed. "Stay a moment. Not Arabella Leighton, the heiress?"

AN INNOCENT IMPOSTER 211

The earl nodded.

With a bark of laughter, Sir Richard slapped his thigh. "If that don't beat the dutch! Here I meant to find this heiress and try my luck at winning her. Instead, I fell head over ears in love with a woman I thought was penniless, and she turns out to be that very heiress!"

"Most amusing," agreed the earl politely.

"I daresay, when it comes time to step into parson's mousetrap, fate has a way of putting the perfect female right under a man's nose," continued Sir Richard.

The earl made no reply to this, but it gave him pause to stop and think. If what Sir Richard had said was correct, fate had certainly been busy on his behalf. Miss Layne's lovely face danced before him. Why was he being such a fool? She was lovely, she was kind, she was a woman of character and principle . . . and if he didn't have the opportunity to kiss her soon he would, indeed, go mad! "I am sure the ladies miss us by now," he said. "We should return to them."

Sir Richard was only too happy to agree.

The look Arabella gave Sir Richard when the gentlemen reentered the room left no doubt as to her feelings.

Lord Mayfield looked to see if he could read the same expression in Miss Layne's face. Unfortunately, she lowered her gaze before he had the opportunity.

Well, if he had seen any sign of regard

there, it would have been a miracle, for she had every right to despise him. He had treated her despicably, never believing her, consistently saying unkind things to her. She must think him a monster, indeed. In fact, had she not called him a monster?

His situation did not look hopeful. Mayfield sighed inwardly and wondered what he was going to do to improve it.

Susan watched her "twin" flirting happily with Sir Richard and felt a stab of envy. How she wished Lord Mayfield would look at her the way Sir Richard looked at Arabella. Life seemed so terribly unfair sometimes! Here Miss Leighton would return to London, to her fine gowns and exciting life, and with the gentleman of her choice anxious to marry her while she, Susan Layne, would return to Crawley . . . to do what? It seemed to her as if she had come full circle, for that was the very thing she had been worrying about when the Earl of Mayfield dragged her off to London. For only a moment she allowed herself to wish that Miss Leighton had never been found.

The party finally split up, each going to his or her room, and Susan pulled on her nightshift— Miss Leighton's nightshift, really— determined to take the first coach to Crawley the next day but hoping some miracle would occur to prevent her. Perhaps the

AN INNOCENT IMPOSTER

Earl of Mayfield would come to her and . . . What? She was not sure what. An earl would never offer for a poor little nobody. But if he would only kiss her. Just one kiss to live on happily the rest of her life. That would be nice. She climbed into bed, taking the pleasant dream with her.

The spring chill the next morning was a cold dose of reality, parting Susan from her pleasant dreams. She dressed and hurried downstairs, telling herself that her haste was simply because she was anxious to find something hot to drink to warm herself.

As she came downstairs she encountered Mrs. Dickens, who looked her up and down. "And which one are you?"

"I am Miss Layne."

"Well, the earl is in the private dining room. He said if I saw you to send you in. Such goings on," the woman muttered as Susan hurried down the hallway.

She found the earl standing before the fire. He turned at the sound of the door and smiled at her. "Miss Layne?"

She nodded.

"Do come join me at the fire," he offered.

Susan came and reached her cold hands to the flame.

"Rather chilly this morning, is it not?" he observed.

She nodded.

"I thought, after the last few days that we were on to warmer weather," he continued, "but it would appear we have a few cold spring mornings still left to endure."

"It would appear that way," Susan agreed.

The earl pressed his lips together and Susan waited while he considered what to say next. "Miss Layne," he said at last, "you must allow me to make up for the hardship I have caused you."

"I told your lordship before, that is not necessary," said Susan stiffly.

"Yes, I know, but I truly wish to show my gratitude."

Gratitude. That was all he felt. Susan blinked hard, determined to keep the tears at bay. She felt him watching her and turned her face away.

"Miss Layne, I must ask you a very great favor," he said suddenly.

"And what is that?" she asked in a tight voice.

"That you return to London with us."

To London? Stay with the Earl of Mayfield? But why would he wish such a thing? "I am afraid I don't understand," said Susan.

"It is . . ." He paused, his brows furrowed. "Because of my ward I ask. You see, I am afraid somehow word might get out that she has been staying here at The Swan, for all purposes unchaperoned. It would ruin her. But," he said slowly, then stopped.

Susan looked at him, waiting.

He snapped his fingers and continued in

a rush, "If you were to return with us, we could say you are Arabella's cousin from Crawley come to visit. Then no one need ever know it wasn't Arabella who was in London all this time."

This all seemed rather lame to Susan. No one would ever know anyway. "Surely your lordship is worrying needlessly," she said.

"Oh, I don't think so," said Mayfield. "Please, Miss Layne. Say you will come. I am sure we can make your stay enjoyable."

What else had she to look forward to? "Very well," she said. "If your lordship wishes it."

"I do wish it," replied Mayfield.

He seemed at a loss for what to say next, and the smile he gave Susan looked suspiciously like a nervous one. How very odd, she thought. And how different from the strong-minded man who had hauled her to London against her will.

Now he was taking her to London again. And this time she was going willingly. Why? she asked herself. Why are you doing this? What do you hope will come of it?

"Good morning," sang Lady Mayfield, strolling into the room. "I vow, only birds should be up this early."

The earl turned and went to greet his mother. The nervousness Susan had just seen fell from him and he was once again the same confident man she knew. "Having gone to bed with the birds, Mother, I imagine it was no difficult thing to wake up with them," he teased.

Lady Mayfield frowned. "Why we must start back at such a ridiculous hour, Gerard, I cannot imagine. Of course, what else there might be to do here I cannot imagine, either."

"There you have it," said her son. "Besides, are you not anxious to return to London and introduce Arabella's cousin, Miss Layne, into polite society?"

Lady Mayfield looked thoughtfully, first at the earl, then at Susan.

Susan stole a glance at him and saw a red stain creeping up his neck. "I thought it would scotch any scandal," he said. "And I think it only fair we allow Miss Layne to finish out the season."

"I certainly agree," said her ladyship. She smiled at Susan. "After all we have put you through I should say it is the least we can do, my dear."

Susan remembered a certain conversation she'd had with Lady Mayfield. Was her ladyship playing Cupid?

Arabella was the next to enter the room. Susan noticed that, although she was wearing a very nice blue muslin gown she eyed Susan's suspiciously. "I am afraid I am wearing yet another of your gowns," Susan apologized.

"Arabella can spare a gown or two," said Lord Mayfield, which made his ward frown.

"Miss Layne will be accompanying us to London," he informed her. "People are bound to remark on the amazing resemblance. If anyone cares to know, she is your cousin from Crawley."

"But I haven't a cousin in Crawley," protested Arabella. "Have I?"

"I believe you do," said the earl.

At that moment Sir Richard joined them and Arabella was too distracted by his presence to question the earl further.

After a leisurely breakfast, the company left, the ladies riding in the Mayfield carriage, the gentlemen following on horseback. For most of the trip Arabella was pleasant company, planning her future with glee, unknowingly adding to Susan's misery. At one point she made reference to the fact that her twin had enjoyed a life of ease and pleasure while she had suffered miserably at The Swan.

Lady Mayfield cut her off in mid-complaint. "I might remind you, young lady, that it was your own foolishness that brought you to that sad pass. You may be thankful that Miss Layne is a woman of principle. Another lady would have taken your place and left you to a life of peeling potatoes and scrubbing floors. You may also be thankful that Miss Layne's kindness has earned you more admiration and respect than you had thus far managed to garner on your own. I suggest you behave with propriety and charity the rest of the season and see if you cannot keep the good opinion of others which she has won for you."

Arabella looked wide-eyed at Lady Mayfield, then clamped her lips shut in a pout.

Susan blushed and looked out the window and wondered what on earth she was doing traveling to London with the Earl of Mayfield.

They arrived tired and stiff, and dined quietly at home that night. Arabella, Susan noticed, seemed glad enough to be back, and perfectly happy with her lot in life. Until the earl began to discuss with his mother a shopping expedition to outfit Susan for the following day.

"She has been wearing my gowns the whole time I was gone," hissed Arabella when Childers' back was turned, "and now she is to have new ones?"

The earl rolled his eyes. "Now things are, indeed, back to the way they were," he said.

The following day Lady Mayfield took Susan shopping, Arabella tagging along, taking great pleasure in spoiling Susan's. Susan was sure they visited every dressmaker and milliner in Oxford Street and as the purchases became increasingly more whimsical, she became more nervous. Finally, when Lady Mayfield led them into the shop of W. H. Botibol, plumassier, looking for feathers to adorn a gypsy hat, she felt she must protest. "Surely

AN INNOCENT IMPOSTER

Lord Mayfield did not mean us to purchase so very many things," she said.

"I am sure I have never spent so much in one day," put in Arabella, "and I am rich."

"Nonsense," said Lady Mayfield, picking up a pink ostrich plume.

Susan bit her lip and wondered where this extravagance would all end.

It ended with the purchase of some lemon kid gloves, a fan, and a parasol. At last they returned home, the footman staggering up the walk behind them, laden with packages.

Lady Mayfield and Arabella went up to their rooms to change. Susan, however, asked Childers if the earl was in.

The earl, it seemed, was in the drawing room. Miss Leighton's aunt had arrived, and he was waiting for her to join him there.

Susan hesitated, wondering if this was the best time to tell the earl of the great sum of money that had been drained from his pockets. "Would you care for me to announce you, Miss Leigh . . . Layne?" stumbled Childers.

"No. Thank you," said Susan, suddenly losing her courage. She got halfway to her room before determination sent her hurrying back to the drawing room.

The earl was standing before the hearth. He turned and, at the sight of her, broke into a great smile. Then, as if checking himself, he looked at her carefully. "Miss Layne? It is you, is it not?" She nodded and the smile returned. "Did you enjoy your shopping trip?"

"That is what I have come to speak with you about," said Susan, coming farther into the room.

"Yes?"

"I am afraid your mother got rather carried away when we went shopping today."

"She did so with my full permission," said the earl.

"Oh, but you can have no idea of the amount of money we spent," fretted Susan.

The earl chuckled. "Oh, but I can," he assured her.

Susan was not amused. "I can not, in good conscience, allow you to do so much for me."

"Miss Layne, can you honestly worry about allowing me to do something so small after the great damage I have done you? A day's shopping hardly begins to pay for my crimes."

"You have not damaged me, my lord," said Susan.

"What of your feelings?"

Susan suddenly found great interest in the simple task of clasping her hands in front of her. "I knew everything you said and did while I was with you was not meant for me, but for Arabella."

The earl was looking at her, his expression unreadable. "Not everything," he said. With a look of determination, he closed the distance between them, pulled her to him, and

AN INNOCENT IMPOSTER 221

kissed her savagely. "I am sorry," he whispered against her cheek. "You must forgive me."

"Forgive you?" she managed.

"I have been wanting to kiss you for so very long. I considered myself mad, feeling such a strong attraction for my spoilt ward. All that time you were under my roof I fought it, but I have no desire to fight it any longer. Miss Layne— "

"Susan."

"Susan, please say you will marry me."

She stared at him, hardly able to believe her ears.

"It will make your mother very happy," he added. "And mine, too, I suspect."

"I am only a governess," she said.

"Where is the shame in that?" he said gently. "Many a gently born lady has been a governess."

"Oh, your lordship— "

The earl smiled. "Gerard."

"Gerard," she said shyly. "Are you sure you want to do this?"

"I am as sure of what I want to do as I am of whom I hold," he said, smiling down at her.

The door opened, and a small woman with a plump, lined face and small, blue eyes stepped across the threshold. At the sight of the embracing couple she let out a gasp. "Arabella, my dear!" she scolded feebly. "Lord Mayfield, this is most improper."

"I am afraid you have mistaken my intended for your niece," replied the earl, bringing Susan closer to the little woman. "This is Miss Susan Layne."

"But . . . it cannot be," said the lady, looking at Susan in disbelief.

"The resemblance is remarkable, is it not?" observed the earl.

"Aunt!" cried the real Arabella, skipping into the room. "You have come to visit. And you are just in time to hear of my engagement."

"To Lord Redburrough?" ventured the woman.

"Oh, gracious no," said Arabella, dropping into a chair and curling her feet under her. "This man is much younger and so handsome . . ."

The earl took Susan by the hand and they slipped out of the room. "I suppose we should go and tell my mother the news," he said, stopping to put his arms around Susan once more.

"I suppose we should," she agreed dreamily, and they remained where they were.

"I do hope that in the future you won't have trouble telling Arabella and I apart," Susan teased when they finally went up the stairs arm in arm.

"I shan't," said the earl confidently.

"It would appear that even Arabella's aunt has difficulty in distinguishing between us.

AN INNOCENT IMPOSTER 223

How ... so sure you will have no

...ed and replied, "There are
... dearest love, that a man
..."

ZEBRA REGENCIES
ARE
THE TALK OF THE TON!

A REFORMED RAKE (4499, $3.99)
by Jeanne Savery
After governess Harriet Cole helped her young charge flee to France—and the designs of a despicable suitor, more trouble soon arrived in the person of a London rake. Sir Frederick Carrington insisted on providing safe escort back to England. Harriet deemed Carrington more dangerous than any band of brigands, but secretly relished matching wits with him. But after being taken in his arms for a tender kiss, she found herself wondering—*could* a lady find love with an irresistible rogue?

A SCANDALOUS PROPOSAL (4504, $4.99)
by Teresa DesJardien
After only two weeks into the London season, Lady Pamela Premington has already received her first offer of marriage. If only it hadn't come from the *ton's* most notorious rake, Lord Marchmont. Pamela had already set her sights on the distinguished Lieutenant Penford, who had the heroism and honor that made him the ideal match. Now she had to keep from falling under the spell of the seductive Lord so she could pursue the man more worthy of her love. Or was he?

A LADY'S CHAMPION (4535, $3.99)
by Janice Bennett
Miss Daphne, art mistress of the Selwood Academy for Young Ladies, greeted the notion of ghosts haunting the academy with skepticism. However, to avoid rumors frightening off students, she found herself turning to Mr. Adrian Carstairs, sent by her uncle to be her "protector" against the "ghosts." Although, Daphne would accept no interference in her life, she *would* accept aid in exposing any spectral spirits. What she never expected was for Adrian to expose the secret wishes of her hidden heart . . .

CHARITY'S GAMBIT (4537, $3.99)
by Marcy Stewart
Charity Abercrombie reluctantly embarks on a London season in hopes of making a suitable match. However she cannot forget the mysterious Dominic Castille—and the kiss they shared—when he fell from a tree as she strolled through the woods. Charity does not know that the dark and dashing captain harbors a dangerous secret that will ensnare them both in its web—leaving Charity to risk certain ruin and losing the man she so passionately loves . . .

Available wherever paperbacks are sold, or order direct from the Publisher. Send cover price plus 50¢ per copy for mailing and handling to Penguin USA, P.O. Box 999, c/o Dept. 17109, Bergenfield, NJ 07621. Residents of New York and Tennessee must include sales tax. DO NOT SEND CASH.